T0246561

MURDER
IN THE
HILLS OF
CHIANTI

JACK V EITELGEORGE

Murder in the Hills of Chianti

© Jack V. Eitelgeorge

ISBN 979-8-35094-682-6

eBook ISBN 979-8-35093-242-3

DEDICATION

This book is dedicated to my late wife, Sandra.

She inspired me to become an Italian.

I grew to love all things Italian and to cherish
their peaceful culture.

We can learn much from them.

"You now walk in heaven's light
Surrounded by God's love
With angels song
On the scented air."

—Paul Curtis

CONTENTS

PREFACE.. 1

CHAPTER 1: IT'S BEEN A GOOD TEN YEARS 3

CHAPTER 2: THE DREAMS OF A GENOVESE TYCOON 14

CHAPTER 3: A NIGHTMARE... 30

CHAPTER 4: A WORLD OF MURDER 45

CHAPTER 5: THE MONSTER... 59

CHAPTER 6: THE GREEN LIGHT.................................... 68

CHAPTER 7: SUSPECTS..81

CHAPTER 8: STUNNER.. 96

CHAPTER 9: EPILOGUE..107

ACKNOWLEDGEMENTS 111

PREFACE

"Murder in the Hills of Chianti" is a sequel to two earlier books, "The Meat Eaters" and "The Lady From Como." Those stories followed the events in the life of a California attorney who became involved in criminal investigations, testing his ability to rise to formidable challenges.

In this novella, the attorney, Jeff Wiler, is again drawn into a case that forces him to participate in criminal investigations. He thought the need to face dangers was over ten years ago. Now, he takes part in the probe of a murder.

This story takes place mostly in Italy, with the murder of his partner's father-in-law. It follows a decade of peace and prosperity for the Wilers and their family.

This interruption of 'a happy life' demonstrates the fragility of good times. It shows that life has no absolute guarantees. We learn life's lessons as we go, sometimes after a particular tragedy. We call it wisdom. We hope we receive it through growth and not a major tragedy.

I wrote "The Meat Eaters" as a thesis thirty-two years ago, earning a master's degree in creative writing at California State University-Sonoma. Upon retirement, I revised the work and published it in 2021. In 2022, I wrote "The Lady From Como." And now, "Murder in the Hills of Chianti."

As a home winemaker, I was attracted to the wine region of Chianti. Its romance inspired me to write about it in this latest work.

The book is fiction, seeking to demonstrate strong compassion in an often-heartless world. It portrays a tragedy that requires the protagonists to step up to face the challenges that come before them.

This finishes the trilogy.

These novellas have allowed me to exercise not only my passion for writing but also the opportunity to go back in time and places to describe nostalgic experiences.

Hopefully, this work will demonstrate a degree of positivity. Major threats are unwanted, but sometimes, they allow us to learn true values in life. We cannot ignore obvious injustices, expecting others to rectify them. And as we all have heard, we cannot expect the world to be perfect. It is fragile.

We all need to exercise reconciliation and forgiveness. We must do more than just apologize for unkind behavior. We must remedy it.

I was born and raised in Vallejo, California. I studied Italian, and ten years ago attained Italian citizenship. So, with my writing and my love of Italy, I can write stories that are fiction but contain certain histories, truths, and facts.

With my California life and my Italian experiences, I can relive those wonderful years through fiction.

The beauty of aging is the chest of treasured memories.

Jack V. Eitelgeorge—October 2023

CHAPTER 1

IT'S BEEN A GOOD TEN YEARS

On Friday, businessman Curt Baker was returning to his small home on Cooper's Lane in Grand Haven, Michigan, after attending a week-long insurance marketing seminar in Chicago. Although it was after midnight when he flew into Chicago, he wanted to sleep in his own bed and relax for the weekend. Having divorced two years ago, he regarded his home as his haven—quiet and relaxing.

He probably should have stayed in a Chicago hotel and driven the 100 miles home the next day, but he was anxious to get home and chose to put the two-hour drive behind him.

As he parked his car in his driveway, he sighed and thought, "Finally here." He walked in the front door to see total darkness inside.

"Nuts," he muttered. His security night light had gone out. As he entered the entrance hall, he placed his suitcase and briefcase on the floor, then heard a slight sound, a 'click' behind the kitchen door. Then came another 'click.'

Was it the refrigerator? Was it an animal? Or worse?

He slowly crept across the living room toward the kitchen. There was no light showing under the door. He quietly grasped the door handle and slowly pushed the door inward. Suddenly, . . .

"Jeff, could you come and help me?"

Startled, Jeff Wiler jerked in his chair, then laid his mystery novel on the side table of the den. His wife Sofia walked into the room to ask the question again.

Sofia is the light of Jeff's life. Their romantic marriage is a story of grandeur. And his life, in many ways, was a happy fairy tale.

So why would a content, moderately wealthy middle-aged lawyer in California trade the easy life with all its comforts to bury himself in the dangerous position of investigating a murder in Italy?

In the summer of 1982, Jeff Wiler did just that—his sense of daring came alive when he was faced with a risky challenge. And this was not the first time—nor the second.

After ten peaceful years of lovely marriage, the birth of a beautiful child, and financial success as an attorney, the 43-year-old was ready to step up again.

He recalled with some anxiety the events of over a decade ago when he risked his life prosecuting violent gang members who committed murder. He later worked in 1972 to help capture an international criminal who set up an illegal immigration system for organized crime members to enter the United States. Although that individual was a murder suspect, he was never convicted of that crime. He was sent to federal prison for violating U.S. immigration laws.

Currently, Jeff is a content man. After three or four stressful years, his helter-skelter days of chaos ended a decade ago. He credits Sofia for his happiness.

He had an earlier, rocky marriage of almost ten years, ending in divorce. The couple had married too young, and Jeff was still in college when he became a father. A second child came three years later while he was in law school. His main regret of the split-up was being separated from his two daughters, Suzy and Laurie, especially after his ex-wife moved from Oakland, California, to San Diego, California. As in any such breakup, the children are usually the most adversely affected.

After law school, Jeff was hired as a Deputy District Attorney at the Alameda, California District Attorney's office. He excelled and soon developed an impressive reputation. His competence led to a temporary upgrade to District Attorney.

But his temporary upgrade was not one to celebrate.

His superior, Weldon Duffy, was murdered in a car bombing. The County of Alameda was cracking down on several members of a breakaway branch of the Black Panther Party in Oakland. Some were imprisoned, awaiting trial.

The District Attorney in Alameda County was an elective position, so someone had to temporarily step in for Duffy until the next election over a year later.

It involved a significant degree of danger as Jeff sought to prosecute the Black Panthers in custody. He never would have imagined his assignment would lead to the kidnapping of his daughter, Suzy.

Amazingly, he involved himself in negotiations with the kidnappers and was able to personally rescue Suzy under the threat of being shot.

Although bizarre, that earlier upgrade to temporary District Attorney ended positively. The uprising was quelled, and he gained confidence and a degree of notoriety, being lauded for successfully handling the assignment.

Some people have a hidden resilience that they are unaware of—and then, one day, find themselves in danger of physical harm, including death. From some unknown strength, they receive a resolve that awakens and gives them the power to take charge and defeat the source of the threat.

Other people may not have that inner strength, even if they have physical strength. But inner strength is invisible; it needs a catalyst—some form of physical or mental fortitude. Otherwise, the source of the threat wins.

A couple of years after those unbelievable events, Jeff reconnected with a former law school classmate, Flavio Acquistapace, who came to the Bay Area from Italy with an important assignment. It involved an international investigation—an audit of potential illegal entries into the United States from abroad—primarily Italy. Flavio recruited Jeff to join in the study.

The audit revealed many instances where organized crime members traveled undetected to and from the United States. It provided the Federal Bureau of Investigation and the Italian Polizia with statistical information that enabled law enforcement to break up the illegal immigration activities.

However, the study and follow-up resulted in an intense period of several weeks for Jeff and Flavio. It was a threat by a particularly dangerous gangster named DiCarlo, who was ready to murder them. The two men worked closely with U.S. and Italian law enforcement to bring DiCarlo down. Following those shaky weeks, the two men were ready to settle down and live a "normal" life again.

During that assignment, Jeff entered a relationship with Sofia Acquistapace, Flavio's sister. She worked in tourism in Como, Italy. The beautiful blue-eyed lady was very independent but had been uninterested in a romantic relationship with anyone. She had the type of personality Jeff was drawn to—exciting and challenging. He won her over through his respect for her independence. As it turned out, his attention sparked her interest and trust in romance.

Jeff's marriage to Sofia and his love for her have been the best years of his life. He never knew such happiness could exist. He treasures the past incredible decade that his beautiful blue-eyed wife gave him.

He asks himself daily why this great fortune has been given to him. He and Sofia have never argued.

'How is this possible? How did I find this amazing woman?'

Sofia is still beautiful in every way. Her thick, wavy hair with natural curls cups her beautiful face—much like a picture frame. It is dark with light tones of gray. She has high cheekbones below intense but pleasing blue eyes. Her long neck and slim torso make her appear taller. Her wide smile is ready, with natural lines slightly held back, with composure.

She appears almost unable to frown or show anger. She is naturally confident, with no arrogance of superiority or criticism of others. His attractive wife dresses in a flamboyant yet tasteful way—always beautiful with no apparent effort. Sofia carries herself like a celebrity.

When someone takes her picture, she doesn't look AT the camera—but INTO it. It's the same when she converses with people—she looks directly into their eyes and listens closely.

Occasionally, Jeff thinks, 'I want to hold my breath for as long as possible. This great blessing cannot last forever.'

And she is deeply in love with her man.

They married in California in November of 1972 and chose to live there. Sofia's surname remained Acquistapace, as is the custom in Italy, where women normally maintained their surnames upon marriage. If she followed U.S. tradition and took the last name Wiler, her initials would become 'SOW,' forcing her to endure years of joking comments from friends. She had asked Jeff for his permission to maintain her surname, and laughingly, he consented.

A little over a year following their marriage, a baby girl arrived. She was named Gina. All three were now Italian citizens. Jeff had been able to apply for citizenship following his marriage to Sofia.

Sofia's brother, Flavio, married his Italian lady friend, Celeste Gotelli, in California in 1973. She was an employee he met while investigating travel records at the Italian Consulate. Her parents were Antonio and Caterina Gotelli. Antonio was an industrialist in Genoa, Italy.

Flavio and Jeff eventually formed a law firm in Napa, California, and settled into a quieter lifestyle. When forming their new firm, they agreed that each law case they would take would first be analyzed to ensure there would be no connection to organized crime factions. They had enough of those fears earlier, saying, "We want no case involving gangsters and murderers!"

By now, in May of 1982, success and happiness had followed them.

Each summer, the two men and their families traveled to Italy to spend time with their relatives.

They both loved wine and its popularity in California. But they preferred Italian wines and felt a fascination with them. They had heard certain Italian wines, especially Sangiovese, were successfully competing against the more expensive French wines of the past. The Italians concluded that Sangiovese could successfully compete with Cabernet Sauvignon at a lower cost. Jeff and brother-in-law Flavio had fantasized about making and marketing a high-quality wine one day.

They hoped to pursue the venture when they neared retirement from law practice. When they vacationed in Italy each year, they looked at potential vineyards in Tuscany.

Three years ago, in 1979, Flavio got a call from his dad, Luigi Acquistapace, reporting that a suitable Sangiovese grape vineyard was up for sale. It was near the Castello Brolio, in Chianti (pronounced key-YON-tee), south of Florence, Italy.

Luigi, now retired, had worked many years at the Nino Negri winery near Sondrio, located in northern Italy near the Swiss border.

He was excited when the boys told him earlier that they were interested in entering the wine business one day. He set out to find a suitable vineyard to recommend to them. Chianti was widely known as one of Italy's most desired grape-growing areas, and Sangiovese grapes thrived there. When Luigi learned of a suitable vineyard for sale in that renowned locale, he immediately notified Flavio and Jeff.

They jumped at the opportunity and bought the vineyard. As it worked out, they could employ a neighboring vineyard owner to manage and maintain their vineyard until they retired. Following their venture, their manager kept them updated on the status of the property.

When the men took their families on their annual trips to Italy for a month each summer, they stayed with Sofia and Flavio's parents, Luigi and Gemma Acquistapace, in Piantedo at the north edge of Lake Como. They were Jeff's father-in-law and mother-in-law. This summer of 1982, they chose a two-month vacation to visit the Acquistapaces. They wanted to also to go south and see how their vineyard in Tuscany was doing.

Jeff and Sofia also planned to see more of Italy to enjoy the history and beauty of the country, especially those sites Jeff had never visited. Even Sofia looked forward to seeing other parts of her homeland where she had never been. And they wanted their nine-year-old daughter Gina to continue learning more about the culture of her Italian family.

Jeff's oldest daughter, Suzy, age 21, had grown close to her stepmother, Sofia, being impressed by her independence and her career in tourism. She asked Sofia for her advice on choosing a similar career. Sofia suggested she consider a career that might take advantage of the beauty and charm of the Napa Valley wine country.

Suzy had developed an interest in winemaking and marketing, but all she knew before about wine was the phrase by Orson Wells for Paul Masson of Saratoga, California, in the late 1970s, a motto heard many times on television: "We will sell no wine before it's time."

Suzy enrolled in a wine program offered at the University of California at Davis and took a few classes in winemaking.

It appeared to be an excellent fit for her. Earlier, she had met and grown fond of some of Sofia's Italian relatives in California: the Acquistapace, Pinoli, Deghi, and Pedroncelli families, of whom she had grown fond. Their knowledge of grape growing and winemaking inspired her. She thought a career in the business would be interesting, even glamorous.

She eventually wanted to become a tour guide and expert in the wine business in California. An essential part of her goal was to learn everything about both Californian and Italian wines.

After the UC Davis classes, Suzy could enroll in a six-week wine program at the Accademia del Vino di Firenze in Florence, Italy. She believed that learning all aspects of the wine business, especially from the European point of view, would bolster her resume, and help her launch a successful career in California.

She enrolled in the seminar from May 17th through June 25th, 1982, ending the weekend of Jeff and Sofia's arrival for their annual vacation. They planned to visit her briefly in Florence before she returned to the United States on Monday, June 28th. They were happy to support her because the experience in Italy would be good training for her future career in the wine and tourism business.

Their other daughter, Laurie, age 18, lived in San Diego, California, with her mom, Rita, Jeff's ex-wife. Laurie planned to enter college in California in the coming Fall.

Flavio and his wife Celeste originally planned to join Jeff and his family in Florence for a few days, then go see Celeste's Genovese relatives, the Gotellis, in Genoa. They would meet up with Jeff and Sofia again later while there.

Before traveling, Flavio wanted to ensure their employee, Donato Cuneo, was ready to run the law firm by himself for the summer months. Donato, an Italian attorney, joined the firm just six months ago. A competent lawyer, he had helped Flavio land a special investigation assignment at the Italian consulate in San Francisco ten years earlier.

During their vacation, Jeff and Flavio also wanted to visit their dear friend Amadeo Mattaruchi, the Italian police chief who helped them following the car bombing incident in Milan in 1972 when organized crime members threatened them.

They had become close and remained friends for over a decade. In each annual visit to Italy, they contacted Mattaruchi for a visit, usually in Milan, just 65 miles from Piantedo, where their family lived.

In the United States, they also occasionally connected with the Federal Bureau of Investigation Supervising Agent Frank Fargo, who had worked closely to support them during those frantic, chaotic times a decade earlier. They saw him often because he was in the States and was semi-retired. He was a seasoned investigator and still served as an advisor for the FBI and an instructor for new agents. He dropped in on Flavio and Jeff in the United States from time to time to visit.

Fargo had earlier introduced the two men to Mattaruchi, his Italian counterpart. Those two police leaders guided the two men when dealing with organized criminals. That stressful period was why Jeff and Flavio pledged to avoid future cases involving organized crime. Jeff and Flavio were grateful to them.

But they knew a case would probably come up someday where an organized crime member had some such involvement.

Over the years, Mattaruchi had remained their hero and friend. They thanked him each year for his wonderful support ten years earlier. The threats and chaos of 1972 created lasting bonds between the men.

Shortly before their upcoming vacation, a concerning telephone call changed their plans.

On Tuesday, June 22, 1982, just before they were to leave for Italy, Jeff received a call from Suzy. She sounded shaken and reported that there had been a murder in Florence three days ago by a serial killer. The victims had been young people murdered at night in a remote area outside the city. Known as the Monster of Florence, he had killed several people over the past few years. Suzy said she was afraid and would not go out at night— unless they caught the killer.

She called to find out how soon the family was coming to see her. She had become afraid of being alone in Italy without her family.

She had gone out on a dinner date in the city with an Italian class-mate who had flirted with her a few times. After dinner, the young man, Giovanni Mazzina, took a longer way home. He pulled over on a rural road and asked that they "just chat to get to know each other better." Suzy saw through all that and insisted he drive her back to her school dorm. There was no opposition, and the young man did as she instructed.

A day or so later, the newspaper La Nazione in Florence announced a murder near the road on which the young man had chosen to take Suzy.

* * *

The news article read in detail:

Double Murder in the Galluzzo Neighborhood

On Saturday, 19 June 1982, between ten and eleven o'clock p.m., mechanic Paolo Mainardi, age 22, and dressmaker Antonella Migliorini, age 20, were shot in Mainardi's car on a provincial road in Montespertoli. Several passing motorists had seen the car parked at the side of the road after its interior light had turned on and notified the police.

Antonella died at the crime scene. Mainardi was still alive when found but later died in the hospital due to serious injuries.

The killer had driven Mainardi's car for a few meters to hide the vehicle and the bodies in a woodland area nearby, only to lose control of the car and abandon it in the ditch, where it was discovered by a motorist who stopped to investigate.

The victims' families have been notified, and an investigation is underway.

Police believe the murders were the work of The Monster of Florence.

✶   ✶   ✶

Upon reading this, Suzy was frightened and called home.

Jeff tried to console her, giving a few dos and don'ts such as always traveling with other people when out, not going to dark or risky places, always letting people know where she was, and so forth—not tremendously reassuring, but normal for a father to say. He also moved their departure day up a few days earlier, promising to contact her as soon as they arrived.

He called her each morning for the next few days so she would hear from him before darkness came in Italy—a nine-hour time difference. He wanted to assure her that they would be there soon. The calls eased her fear, knowing that the family would soon be with her.

Could this summer vacation hold a different agenda for them?

CHAPTER 2

THE DREAMS OF A GENOVESE TYCOON

A cunning Italian businessman seeks to make a name for himself in the world of wine. He lives in Genoa, and he has a plan.

In the northern Province of Liguria, Italy, lies the city of Genoa, Italy, about 14 hours by airplane from San Francisco. The province is unique in its size and proximity to the sea. Liguria has little space for cities and streets because it is mostly on a slope. But Genoa's location on the sea has contributed to its greatness over the years. It is a city of many personalities. It is the largest old town in Europe. An old town is an original historical part of a modern city protected from further development.

It is a major center for finance and commerce. The Port of Genoa leads all other Italian ports in the volume of passengers and freight traffic and is the main source of city income.

Genoa is the capital of the Italian region of Liguria and is the sixth-largest city in Italy. It became part of Italy in the 1st century BC when the country was an entity within the Roman State.

It was the capital of one of the most powerful maritime republics for over seven centuries, particularly from the 12th century to the 15th century. The city played a leading role in commercial trade in Europe, becoming one of the largest naval powers of the continent, and it was considered one of the wealthiest cities in the world. Its solid financial sector dates to the Middle Ages.

The Bank of Saint George, founded in 1407, is the oldest known state deposit bank in the world and has played an important role in the city's prosperity.

It was the republic's capital for centuries until 1797, when Napoleon was active militarily throughout Europe. In 1805, Napoleon was crowned King of Italy. After he fell from power, the Genoese State was annexed to the Piedmontite Kingdom of Sardinia. Subsequently, the Kingdom of Sardinia led the Italian unification in 1861.

As most Americans know, Genoa is the birthplace of Christopher Columbus (Cristoforo Colombo), who embodied the active maritime tradition of the city.

Many old landmarks are still in the city today, including the house of Columbo. This remarkable structure still stands almost 500 years after Columbus' famous voyage to the New World. It is a 2-story house built of large stones and brown bricks. The structure is 20 feet wide and 25 feet high, with several patches between the stones.

As a democratic country, Italy is younger than the United States. Of course, as a civilized country, it is hundreds of years older. It dates to pre-biblical times—with many shapes, rulers, invasions, and many 'contortions' to end up the beautiful country it is today.

Like the United States, each region of Italy has its own unique identity—its cuisine, climate, geography, history, and diversity. Each province of the Italian Republic comprises many municipalities (comunita). Several provinces together form a region; the region of Aosta Valley is the sole exception—it is not subdivided into provinces, and the region exercises provincial functions.

Genoa has a very important story as a Maritime Republic city-state, which also had some 'foreign' territories at some points in its history—at one time, the island of Corsica.

Most people do not know that Genoa and Liguria are among the oldest territorial entities in post-Roman Italy. The Republic of Genoa became autonomous in the Eleventh Century and existed as an independent state for seven centuries.

At one point, it was one of the world's richest maritime powers and one of Europe's most important banking and financial centers—a probable factor behind the Ligurians' historical reputation as stingy or 'tight' people.

In modern times, Genoa became an industrial city. There are several essential industries there, including those that produce petroleum, textiles, iron and steel, locomotives, paper, sugar, cement, chemicals, fertilizers, and electrical, railway, and marine equipment. Genoa also is a major center for finance and commerce.

Today, it is a city overflowing with character and charm. Its long history as an independent state led to its distinctive and unmistakable features. For example, Liguria is known for its tall, narrow houses with green gables and fishing towns facing the sea. They were often built on steep hill slopes due to a lack of space. But also impressive are the rich and colorful old aristocratic residencies of Genoa's city center, such as Palazzo Rosso.

Due to its proximity to the Mediterranean Sea, Genoa had become a leader in maritime industries—the most prominent was shipbuilding. Among the most successful companies was the Cantiere Nazionale Italiano, CNI, established over a hundred years ago.

* * *

CANTIERE NAZIONALE ITALIANO —ITALIAN NATIONAL SHIPYARD

CNI shipyard employs about 120 people and is located close to the Genoa city center and the airport, ensuring customers a range of hotels within walking distance and easy access, saving time and money. It can handle the largest vessels and is ideally positioned to support all the maritime sector's needs, providing specialized services and emergency assistance any day of the year.

In the early years, the shipyard was primarily focused on routine maintenance and repair operations—on-site in Genoa. Today, it has a staff of naval mechanical engineers, skilled workers, emergency response teams, and specialized technicians. So now, it not only builds ships with varying specifications but can also send personnel to repair disabled vessels worldwide.

Then, the firm eventually entered the glorious post-war decade in the 1950s.

Modern-day ships are much larger than those built a hundred years ago. They are made of metal—a big difference from earlier times. Shipbuilding and maintenance became far more demanding than in the days of wooden ships. Metal has allowed ships to be much larger and more durable, but it requires major building and maintenance. Among the modern technologies came metal carpentry, simply building with metal rather than wood.

These advancements enabled CNI to broaden its scope and be able to repair and upgrade ships at other locations around the globe. This lent to its ongoing success.

And it provided a long and successful career for Antonio Gotelli.

* * *

Gotelli is a vice president for CNI. The current president is his cousin, Roberto Gotelli, who is younger than him. His uncle, Cristoforo Gotelli, had been president of the corporation and retired two years ago. The top position then fell to Cristoforo's son, Roberto.

Although Antonio is a part of Cristoforo's family, he had to work his way up to his present level in the firm. His success was not due to favoritism—he earned the vice presidency through determination and many extra hours put in over the years. He counted his blessings for his success. In his mind, he owed a lot to CNI. It had been a good career fit for him.

An outsider might characterize him as a successful, strong businessman—and he is. But he has a shrewd and often ruthless side to him. He knows what he wants and will take whatever means are needed to succeed.

Born in 1920, he loved his native Genoa, where he lived all his life. However, in 1945, at age 25, while stationed in Milan in the military, he met and married his present wife, Caterina, who was two years older than him. Coincidentally, their marriage and honeymoon happened at the same time as the assassination of Benito Mussolini.

* * *

Benito Amilcare Andrea Mussolini (1883 – 1945) was voted out of power by the Italian Grand Council on July 25, 1943, and imprisoned in a prison on the island of La Maddalena. The prison is famous for being Mussolini's incarceration between August 28 and September 12, 1943, following the Armistice of Cassibile.

The Armistice of Cassibile was signed on 3 September 1943, and made public on September 8, between the Kingdom of Italy and the Allies of World War II. It was an agreement signed at a conference of generals from both sides in an Allied military camp at Cassibile in Sicily, which the Allies had recently liberated.

The armistice presented a total capitulation of Italy and was approved by both King Victor Emanuel III and Prime Minister Pietro Badoglio.

On September 12, 1943, before the Allied Invasion of the mainland, Mussolini was rescued by German forces at La Maddalena. For protection, he was taken to the Hotel Campo Imperatore on the slopes of Monte Portella in the Apennines at 6,990-foot elevation in the Region of Abruzzo, east of Rome.

Today, Hotel Campo is the main lodging for the ski resort of the same name and a starting point for hiking on the western side of the Gran Sasso.

When the Allies invaded the mainland of Italy, Mussolini fled north toward Switzerland, but he was stopped by a group of loyalists on the east side of Lake Como. They executed him on April 28, 1945.

* * *

Antonio and Caterina had three adult children: Gianni, Celeste, and Domenico, who were by now adults. But one was from Caterina's first marriage. Gianni, Caterina's son from her first marriage in 1940, was born in 1943. She had been married to Alfonso Musso, who died in 1944.

Daughter Celeste was born in 1946, and son Domenico was born in 1948. Both were children of Caterina's second husband, Antonio Gotelli. Celeste was to later marry a man named Flavio Acquistapace from Piantedo, Italy.

By age 61, Antonio Gotelli was quite wealthy. He had decided to retire early from the high-pressure position of vice president and enter the wine business, seeking an endeavor with less stress. He loved good wine and, over the years, had become fascinated by the wine industry—especially the top-level brands. He believed he could make a successful venture in the wine world by competing against some of the world's prestigious wine companies.

He invited his natural son Domenico to partner in the endeavor, but Domenico, who also worked at CNI, chose to stay there, and continue to work his way up, like his father had done. He earned a bachelor's degree in marine engineering at the University of Genoa in 1970 and had a promising career at CNI. The opportunities of his position far outweighed those of the wine business.

For several years, Gotelli had been particularly interested in wines made from Sangiovese grapes. He thought there was a niche for top-level Italian wines that would challenge the expensive French wines. The successful premium Sassicaia and Ornellaia wines of northern Tuscany inspired him. Unlike the French, Italy used the Sangiovese grape in their premier wines. He believed he could compete against the top premium Italian wines by undercutting the higher-priced ones. His strategy would be to buy two or three promising vineyards, then produce and sell wines below-market prices for a couple of years, drawing customers to him. He was confident he could also produce wines of high quality and garner a sizeable market share. He was willing to pay top prices for vineyards that met his expectations. He welcomed the opportunity to challenge the competition.

He planned to pursue the opportunity to capitalize on the seminal "Super Tuscan" wine, Sassicaia, (Sasso meaning 'stone,' indicating a stony field), which originated in 1948 when first produced by the Incisa Della Rocchetta company, using Cabernet Sauvignon grapes. For years, they made the wine only for family consumption, but a demand for his wine soon developed. The wine company had learned from the French that the rocky terrain produced top wines—a benefit in producing fewer grapes but with higher flavor intensity.

With that knowledge, Gotelli planned to search for small Sangiovese vineyards with rocky soil like those in France and then have some of the vines grafted with Cabernet Sauvignon grapes to complement the Sangiovese. He was confident that he could produce a wine that would challenge Sassicaia and cost less—and he would establish a successful wine business in Chianti with a sizeable market share.

In 1979, he learned that his son-in-law, Flavio Acquistapace, and his partner had purchased an ideal vineyard in Chianti. He knew the vineyard would produce premium grapes since it was in a renowned growing area. That might fit into his plan nicely.

He planned to establish reduced prices for his wines at first, as he could withstand a temporary loss while acquiring the vineyards and establishing his winery. He knew it would take time to build the operation but felt it would be successful in the long run. He was confident he would eventually succeed in the land of enchantment, Tuscany.

*　*　*

Italy has twenty regions, one of which is Tuscany (Toscana). The capital of the region is Florence, Italy. Tuscany has always been known for its beautiful landscapes, history, artistic legacy, and influence on high culture. It is regarded as the birthplace of the Italian Renaissance and has been home to many figures influential in the history of art and science.

One of Italy's greatest legacies is its production of excellent wines. Within Tuscany, there are numerous wine-producing locations. One of the most popular is Chianti, the name of an area between Florence and Siena. The wines there had been produced for hundreds of years.

But the name 'Chianti' then referred only to the growing area, not the wine. The area was officially established in 1716 near the villages of Gaiole, Castellina, and Radda. It was named after the Monti del Chianti ("Chianti Mountains").

Over time, the production area expanded and became nestled in the hills south of Florence and north of Siena. It became famous for producing exclusive wines superior to those produced in other Tuscany localities.

The first known use of the word 'Chianti' as a wine was in 1833, referring to the dry red wine from that specific area in that Tuscany region.

In the mid-to-late 19th century, Baron Bettino Ricasoli (later the Prime Minister of the Kingdom of Italy) helped establish Sangiovese as the blend's dominant grape variety, creating what is today's Chianti wines.

It was originally bottled in traditional squat glass bottles enclosed in a straw basket, called a 'fiasco' (flask). However, currently, those wines are bottled in modern standard-shaped wine bottles.

In 1932, the Chianti area was completely redrawn and divided into seven sub-areas. Some of the villages in those areas then added 'In Chianti' to their names. They identified with their own unique DOC.

* * *

DOC stands for – Denominazione di Origine Controllata (controlled designation of origin). It specifies that the vineyards and the cellars in which the wines are aged are within a certain region. The certification dictates the number of grapes used, the minimum alcohol content, and aspects of the aging process. The designation is important in regulating wine production with high standards. It is beneficial to the wine industry.

* * *

Today, the best examples of Chianti Classico come from a small group of villages located from Siena in the south to the hills below Florence—excellent growing locations due to the region's warm climate and clay-baked soils.

Only Chianti wines from this sub-zone may display the famous Black Rooster seal on the neck of the bottle. It specifies the production area and methods for each wine and guarantees the quality standard of certain wines that pass a government taste test.

The Black Rooster, a historic symbol of the League of Chianti, became the symbol of the wines of Chianti Classico. It is linked to a medieval legend during the hostilities between Firenze and Siena over control of that territory. Mostly, they were battles over the boundaries of each other's territory. The most famous was the Battle of Montaperti in the year 1260, with other, more minor skirmishes since then, keeping each side honest.

With time, the intensity of the hatred diminished, but there remained some mistrust between the sides. So, to bring peace and define the political boundaries between the two cities, they found a mutually agreeable solution.

It was decided that two knights would depart from their respective cities one day at sunrise and meet at the midpoint between the two city-states. That point would then be the agreed-upon boundary.

The signal was to be a rooster's crow at dawn in each of the two cities. It was the agreed-upon signal for each knight to start riding. The Sieneses picked a white rooster; the Florentines chose a black rooster.

Beforehand, the Florentines placed their rooster in a small, dark chicken coop and didn't feed it for a couple of days. Then, very early on the morning of the ride, the black rooster was freed. It began to crow before dawn, allowing the Florence knight to depart well ahead of the Sienese knight.

The Florentine knight met his opponent in Fonterutoli, beyond the midpoint between the cities. This allowed Firenze to control nearly the entirety of the Chianti territory.

*   *   *

Chianti wine is a dominant force in Tuscan viniculture. Many people have heard of the Chianti Classico DOC zone. Not only does it produce great wines, but it's also the second-largest appellation zone in the world after Bordeaux.

A famous wine operation in Tuscany is Il Castello di Brolio of Barone Ricasoli near Gaiole in Chianti. Located on top of an isolated hill a few kilometers from Gaiole, it dominates the southern Chianti Classico countryside. It is one of the impressive defensive castles that guarded Gaiole during battles between Florence and Siena several centuries ago.

Established in 1141, many people find it hard to believe there could be a winery that is over ten centuries old. The Ricasoli family defined the Chianti Classico, and Il Castello di Brolio remains one of the premier estates today.

The castle has always been under the influence of Florence and used as one of its strategic outposts. Because of this, the castle was besieged and destroyed many times over the centuries. Every time, it has been reconstructed following the style of the current age. It suffered its last attack during World War II, as can be noticed by the holes left by shrapnel all over the facade.

The Ricasoli wine is a dry, full-bodied red wine made from local black Sangiovese grapes and white Trebbiano grapes. Wines from the subdistrict of Classico are marked with a black rooster, Gallo Nero, on the label. There are some 250 labels in this region.

Jeff and Flavio's vineyard is 20 miles from Siena. It is about 20 kilometers, 12 miles northeast of Siena, the home of the famous Palio horse races, which occur on July 2 and August 16 yearly.

*   *   *

The background of the Palio races is medieval. The town's central piazza was the site of public games, largely combative contests such as boxing matches, jousting, and at one time bullfights. Public races organized by the contrade (neighborhoods) were popular since the 14th century, called palii alla lunga. The people raced throughout the whole city.

In 1590, when the Grand Duke of Tuscany outlawed bullfighting, the contrade began to organize races in the Piazza del Campo. There were first races on buffalo-backs, then on donkey-back. Then later it became horse racing.

The first modern Palio (called palio alla tonda) took place in 1633.

*   *   *

The centuries-old tradition of Italian winemaking was about to change in the twentieth century.

Marquis Incisa della Rocchetta (10/23/1867—1/5/1931) was the first to decide that the regulations would no longer limit him and that he would begin to explore new territory. With the help of famous enologist Giacomo Tachis, he produced Sassicaia, the precursor of the Super Tuscan variety. Super Tuscans are red wines that do not adhere to traditional blending laws for the region.

The Marquis developed the wine with the knowledge that he had excellent cards in his hand. The vineyards in the Bolgheri region in northern Maremma, where Sassicaia was produced, have characteristic rocky ground very similar to the terrain of Bordeaux. This made the land perfect for the growth of international grapes of outstanding quality, such as

Cabernet Sauvignon and Cabernet Franc, perfect for producing excellent, long-lasting, and structured red wines.

The Italians were matching the French.

One wine is Solaia (pronounced so − lī − ya), "a place where the sun's energy radiates." The name's provenance comes from a hill vineyard in Tuscany, ideally angled to capture the full sun's energy. Solaia began its life as an experiment. In 1978, Italy's Marquis Lodovico Antinori wine organization had a surplus of Cabernet Sauvignon and Cabernet Franc, so they added it to 80% Sangiovese and came up with the Super Tuscan, Solaia.

Gotelli had done extensive research on soil and climate conditions throughout Tuscany. He then targeted a zone near Gaiole in Chianti as the best area that fit his criteria to suit his quest. Some of the best Super Tuscans come from that region. It is a location with limestone soils plus plenty of sun and rain to produce high-quality wines.

Gotelli was sure his plan would open a greater market and increase the demand for the lower-priced Solaia—hopefully a successful new business for him upon retirement. He was a man of high confidence and had no doubts about his ability to succeed. Those who knew him had seen his aggressiveness once he set a business goal. Ruthless behavior in business can sometimes involve a person taking advantage of loyal customers, or competitors in the name of success—forget about the respect of your customers, competitors, or even your employees.

Some of his critics were subordinates who worked with Gotelli at CNI. One likened him to the character played by Zachary Scott in the 1948 movie, "Ruthless:"

"He is a manipulative, megalomaniac businessman whose Midas touch in monetary matters is paired with a limitless inability to build enduring or meaningful relationships with fellow humans. It is said he wasn't a man; he was a way of life!"

"One man's hero is another man's tyrant," another said.

* * *

On May 1, 1982, Gotelli traveled to Florence hoping to find a realtor to help him locate an available vineyard for sale. At that time, Italy was in the throes of the 'Anni di Piombo' (Years of Lead), a term used to describe the period of social and political turmoil in Italy that lasted from the late 1960s into the late 1980s. It was marked by a wave of both far-left and far-right incidents of political terrorism—and the Italian economy was not good.

Since he wanted a property in Chianti, he was advised to contact a reputable realtor in Radda-in-Chianti, just 31 miles south of Florence. He was given the name of Enrico Furielli, who had a good reputation, was honest, and was very familiar with grape-growing properties in Chianti. Gotelli looked him up.

He explained that he was looking for a suitable property in Chianti, preferably near Gaiole, near the Castello di Brolio—an area that matched the soil and climate, like that of French wine-producing areas. Furielli elected to give Gotelli his full attention. He immediately began a search for a promising property for him.

After learning the details of Gotelli's plan, the realtor found a property that would fit his goal. He knew of an elderly grower, Castagno, who passed away recently and had no family, only his widow who still lived there. She was open to selling the property. Furielli told her about a possible bidder. She then requested that her sister and her sister's husband be present to help her with questions and decisions. They would come from Rome, where they would be relocating her.

After Furielli's presentation, professional explanations, and response to questions, she was open to selling the property. The three family members adjourned to decide on an asking price. The vineyard of three hectares, roughly 7.4 acres, with a small house, was offered for 15,000 lire (about 8,500 euros). Without blinking, Gotelli offered 10,000 euros. The offer was immediately accepted. The woman was allowed a month to vacate.

Gotelli had his vineyard. For him, this was fine, as he wasn't in a hurry, and he could take his time to find a second vineyard to buy later.

Gotelli first visited his new vineyard near the Brolio Castle a couple of times on his own and "got to know" the farmers and the terrain. When he first met some of them, he sold himself as a gentleman farmer pursuing a hobby—not a threat.

But the second time, on June 1, he encountered farmer Bruno Pellegrini, who knew the realtor. Earlier Furielli had inadvertently mentioned to Pellegrini that Gotelli intended to buy up property, replant grape varietals, and produce wines like the French-style Super Tuscans, essentially creating a monopoly of sorts—with wines more prestigious than the traditional ones made in the area. It was his goal to upgrade the Sangiovese grape wines.

Farmer Pellegrini was angry about Gotelli's plans, an outsider coming in and changing the traditional agricultural harmony there. Cooperation between the growers would be threatened. Pellegrini then confronted Gotelli and told him he was not welcome there.

Gotelli, a capitalist at heart, brushed him off rather rudely. He had bought the one property and was now looking for another—and had all but said it was "every man for himself."

Pellegrini said, "Va bene, arrogante imbroglione genovese! Sarai dispiaciuto! ("Okay, you arrogant, Genovese crook! You will be sorry!"). And he stomped to his truck and sped away, flipping up stones. He drove straight to the real estate office of Enrico Furielli in Radda. He marched into the realty office and cursed at him for helping Gotelli buy the vineyard.

He yelled, "Furielli, you traitor. You brought that crook Gotelli onto our land just to make a bunch of money! Now that jackass is trying to run us out of business! We hope you are happy. From now on, you are not welcome in our area anymore. We'll show you and your rich friend how tough we can be! Get your money from someone else. We don't want you around!"

Pellegrini then turned and slammed the door on the way out.

The realtor had not said a word. But he called Gotelli and informed him about the incident.

Gotelli was not intimidated. On his next visit to Chianti, he would be ready to take on anyone who challenged his actions. He could care less about "violating" the pact that the local grape growers had to stick together and support one another.

He was planning on another trip two weeks later.

His wife Caterina had said, "Don't go there today, something bad seems imminent."

He only replied, "Nonsense, I'm going. It's not my problem if Pellegrini can't stand competition. There's room for all of us!"

Caterina raised her hands and walked to another room, slowly shaking her head.

He just watched her, with a hint of doubt.

He should have listened to her, and not his instincts.

CHAPTER 3

A NIGHTMARE

The soft rays of early evening twilight bathed the vineyards near the Brolio Castle on June 26th. The castle occupies a strategic hilltop located about 20 miles northeast of Siena. A light summer rain falls, with occasional lightning streaks and the rumble of thunder. The vineyard workers have gone to their homes with upbeat feelings about the harmless rainfall. It is not unusual for rain to fall in Tuscany in June. Sometimes as much as three inches fall in two weeks. Most families in the area have finished their evening meals and are relaxing before bedtime. They do not distinguish the six gunshots of a firearm that coincide with the cracks of thunder—perhaps warnings of the dangers of darkness.

As night falls, most farmers go to bed thinking of the early morning that will beckon their awakenings. A few will witness a grim discovery when they go to their vineyards. They shook their heads when they heard of the official report.

* * *

DEATH NOTICE

Death of Antonio Gotelli, son of Giovanni Carlo Gotelli

Firenze, Toscana, Italia, Civil Registration Records

Gaiole – Castagneto Carducci –Province of Siena

Atti di Morte – 1982

Record # 34 of the year.

Recorded in the year 1982, day two of July at hour 15 (3:00 p.m.), in the City Hall. "I, (attorney) Roberto Rossi, mayor official of the Civil State of the city of Castagneto Carducci, having received from the supervisor of the police notice today relating to the death-bringing to my attention, to enter into the documents of our records, acknowledging that at the hour nineteen (7:00 p.m.) of the day twenty-six of June in the rural village of Gaiole, the death of Antonio Gotelli, resident of Genoa, age 62, business-man, born and living in Genova, husband of the living spouse, Caterina Gotelli. Death by homicide.

Signed by the city official, Agosto Cappelli

* * *

In the wine country of Napa, California, a family was preparing for a much-anticipated vacation to Italy, which included a visit to the Chianti wine country.

Jeff Wiler and his wife Sofia had planned to fly to Florence to see Suzy off on a flight home following her completion of the wine seminar on June 25, and then drive up to Piantedo north of Lake Como, to await the arrival of brother-in-law Flavio and his wife Celeste. After a week in Piantedo, the two families would split up for separate vacations with friends and family. Flavio and Celeste wanted to spend time with Celeste's family in Genoa.

Jeff, Sofia, and 9-year-old daughter Gina had originally planned a two-month visit to see Sofia's parents and explore more of the country they adored. They hoped to expose Gina to more of the culture of Italy. They went to Italy yearly, but this trip would be their longest yet. Gina was especially excited because Grandma Gemma told her she would teach her how to cook Italian style, especially pasta with the North's creams—not the South's style with red tomato sauce. It was essential to the couple that the youngster learn more about the Italian language and culture.

But two days before leaving, Jeff received a frantic call from Flavio. He had appalling news—there had been a murder the day before at the family's vineyard near Castello Brolio, southeast of Florence near Gaiole. The neighbor vineyardist, Bruno Pellegrini, had told Flavio that the murder victim was Flavio's father-in-law, Antonio Gotelli!

It was shocking to all members of the two families. What were they to do now?

The vacation plans of both couples were about to change.

Jeff immediately confirmed the plan to fly to Florence to see Suzy off and then check out the murder site at the vineyard. Flavio and his wife decided to first go directly to Genoa to comfort her widowed mother and plan the family funeral. Then possibly Flavio would join him in Florence a few days later.

They planned to travel to the murder site near their vineyard near Gaiole and determine what actions to take. Surely it would include working with law enforcement.

But Jeff's priority was to meet with Suzy first and ensure she safely boarded her plane home following the wine seminar. He knew the vineyard murder would be especially shocking to her, considering the earlier murder in Florence. She was anxious to travel home.

On Sunday, June 27, when Jeff, Sofia, and Gina arrived in Florence, they went to see Suzy immediately. They confirmed that her flight home the next day was still on schedule. Their arrival reassured her, but she was still eager to return home. They drove her to the airport the next morning and saw her safely off. That evening Jeff called her and confirmed that she was safely at home. She was upbeat and happy to be home. She assured her dad that she would be fine.

Then later that evening, Jeff received another call from Flavio, who told him he would join them in Florence a couple of days later, on Wednesday morning, June 30. His wife, Celeste, would stay in Genoa to be with her grieving mother.

In the meantime, Jeff rented a 1981 Volkswagen Rabbit Diesel hatchback for the couple of months while in Italy. When he picked up the car, he learned it had only a radio for listening to music. Although still upset by the surprising change of events, he briefly thought about his car at home, his 1972 Pontiac Lemans with its cassette player. He always loved music when he drove, and two months in Europe without his cassette player would normally be a hardship in his mind. "But" he admitted to Sofia, "that should be the worst of my problems."

He also rented a separate car for Sofia to drive with his daughter Gina to be with their Italian family in Piantedo, north of Lake Como.

His priority was for him and Flavio to learn more about the shooting at their vineyard.

Once Flavio arrived, the two men drove 45 miles to the vineyard near the Castello Brolio near Gaiole. They wanted to learn the ramifications of the murder at their vineyard.

Upon arrival at the vineyard, they found things quite sedate. Nothing appeared disturbed. The two men visited with Bruno Pellegrini. the neighboring vineyardist and caretaker of their vineyard. He was the person who reported Gotelli's body to the police on June 26. He confirmed that the body had been on Jeff and Flavio's property, just a few meters from his own vineyard.

Pellegrini described the angry 'run-in' he had had with Gotelli a few weeks earlier and his subsequent visit to the realtor, Enrico Furielli. Following the murder, he had told the police investigators about the confrontation.

Pellegrini was a bit worried, knowing that he might be a suspect, but overall, things seemed peaceful to Jeff and Flavio. They doubted Pellegrini was involved in the murder and felt confident that the vineyard was in good hands. They were a bit concerned, though, that the crime scene was technically on their property. After a couple of hours with Pellegrini, they set out to return to Florence.

On their way back, they elected to drop in on realtor Enrico Furielli's office in Radda to discuss the earlier sale of the vineyard to Gotelli. They wanted to get the realtor's 'take' on the confrontation with Pellegrini. The realtor described the discussion and understood Pellegrini's anger. He had dismissed it as "blowing off steam" and had no grudge.

Then Furielli offered his condolences to the two men and made a surprising comment:

"I feel terrible for the murdered man's young wife. She must have taken the tragedy very hard."

Jeff and Flavio looked at each other with surprise.

Jeff asked, "Did you meet her?"

"No, but I saw her nearby on the three occasions I met with Mr. Gotelli at the vineyard. We just said hello."

Then Flavio asked, "Was she an older woman, about age sixty-plus with long gray hair and kind of stocky?"

"No, not really. This gal was much younger, had short, dark hair, and was quite pretty. She just wandered around while Mr. Gotelli and I tended to business."

The two were puzzled when they drove out of Radda on their way to Florence.

As they drove, Flavio said, "I thought it might be my mother-in-law."

"Do you think Antonio had a girlfriend on the side?" Jeff asked.

"I have no idea, but I wouldn't put it past him!"

*   *   *

Back in Florence, the local police requested Jeff and Flavio both stay a few more days while they sorted out the facts behind the murder. So, they stayed alone in the city while the wives were at their parents' residences.

Sofia and Gina drove to Piantedo to be with their Italian family. Weeks ago, before their vacation, Jeff and Flavio had planned to travel to Milan to visit former Polizia Chief Amadeo Mattaruchi, their longtime friend, whom they met ten years ago on an organized crime case. Little did they know they would be seeing a lot more of him.

Having been instructed to stay in Florence for a while, Jeff contacted Mattaruchi in Milan and filled him in on the current events. With no hesitation, his friend offered to come down from Milan to meet with them. Jeff was happy to be able to see him and seek advice on what might be the best path to take, considering the murder at their vineyard.

Mattaruchi was retired and a widower and had plenty of time on his hands. He still had the interest and ability to assist with occasional investigations and was adept at finding valuable information from a few sources, including informants. He sometimes sent out feelers to undercover contact people to learn critical info.

Flavio, still shaken by the murder of his father-in-law, was permitted to go to Genoa for a couple of days to comfort his wife, Celeste, and attend Gotelli's funeral on July 6, along with Celeste's mother, Caterina, and brothers Domenico and Gianni.

While Jeff remained in Florence, he thought about the mystery woman. He had an idea and telephoned realtor Furielli. He asked him if he knew where Gotelli lodged while in Chianti doing business. Furielli said Gotelli had told him it was the Villa Capannelle in Gaiole.

Villa Capannelle opened in 1974 when businessman Raffaele Rossetti moved to a 16th-century Villa in Gaiole. A vineyard of 8.6 acres was planted using local grapes—Sangiovese, Canaiolo, Colorino, and Malvasia. Also planted were just under five acres of olive trees.

Jeff tucked the information away for the time being. He would investigate the information about the mystery lady later.

In the meantime, he wanted to explore Florence. He had fallen in love with the city because it was much like his beloved hometown of Napa—except for its amazing history and importance. It was in the heart of wine country, the climate was mild, and it was a romantic place to visit. There was something about the beautiful orange tiles on the roofs that were enchanting. And so much rich history.

Of the ten provinces in Tuscany, the most populous is the metropolitan city of Florence with just over a million inhabitants. It has the most towns and villages of all Italian provinces, with 44.

The local police force in each province is the Polizia Provinciale, working out of a station called a 'Questor.' There is one in each of the provincial capitals of Italy, including one in the province of Florence.

★   ★   ★

FLORENCE

"To see the sun sink, drowned in his pink and purple and
golden floods, and overwhelm Florence with tides of color that
makes all the sharp lines dim and faint and turn the solid city
into a city of dreams—is a sight to stir the coldest nature."

Mark Twain

* * *

Florence is the birthplace of the Italian Renaissance. The city dates to 59 B.C. when Julius Caesar turned it into a settlement for veteran Roman soldiers. The city resembled more a military camp than an actual city. Still, it started flourishing at the beginning of the second millennium, and by 1100 AD, it was a powerful city-state.

Florence was the capital of the Kingdom of Italy from 1861 until 1870, when Rome took over.

Jeff was able to see the one attraction he had always wanted to visit: the Statue of David. It is one of the most beautiful sculptures in the world.

Commission for the work was given to Michaelangelo Buonarroti on August 16, 1504. It was sculpted out of a block of marble. Originally some parts were gilded: a garland on the head, the trunk behind the right leg, and the sling.

At 17 feet high and weighing just over six tons, it is 6 ½ feet in diameter at the base. It was completed on January 25, 1504. It was decided that it should be placed at the entrance to Palazzo Vecchio, as an emblem of the strength and independence of the Florentines.

On September 8, 1504, it was revealed to the city, arousing the admiration of all.

Jeff was amazed as he looked up at the masterpiece.

Another prominent landmark icon of Florence is the Ponte Vecchio, Italian for 'Old Bridge'. Built in 1345, it spans over the river Arno with 3 arches, an innovative design for the time. It is easily recognizable with all the shops built on it and the covered passage above it, with a private aerial walkway built for the ruling family, the Medici Family.

Adolph Hitler prevented the destruction of the Ponte Vecchio in World War II. During the war, the German army was occupying the city of Florence. The Allies forced them out of the city at the war's end. When they fled, they destroyed all the bridges—except the Ponte Vecchio. Legend has it that Hitler loved the bridge so much that he instructed his troops not to destroy it. The Ponte Vecchio was left untouched.

Florence has two special 'firsts': It was the first city in Europe with paved streets. And it is where Bernardo Buontalenti invented the famous gelato in the 16th century.

Florence is close to 3,000 miles above the equator and has about 15 hours of daylight in July. Napa, California is about 2,660 miles above the equator, and has about 14 hours.

Jeff was enchanted by the history and beauty of both cities.

⋆　⋆　⋆

Jeff stayed in Florence, after visiting the vineyard, and looked forward to seeing Mattaruchi—the friend of ten years. Mattaruchi had been happy to hear from his two friends and volunteered to go to Florence to discuss the case. It is a 155-mile drive from Milan.

He didn't mention it, but he was pumped up to be helping on a major case. He was an expert at creating an Esprit de Corps—a common spirit among the members of a group that creates enthusiasm, devotion, and strong regard for the honor of the group.

When they met in Florence, Mattaruchi introduced another friend and confidant, Reneo Bianchi, to Jeff and Flavio. Bianchi was the local

Deputy Commissioner – the third highest rank in the police career hierarchy in the city. His rank is also known as Deputy Chief of Police, working under the local Police Commissioner.

In the conversation that ensued, Jeff inquired about the murder in Florence. Bianchi gave the men a run-down of the ongoing investigation of murders by the Monster of Florence, soon to be called simply the 'Monster'. The conversation then turned to the murder at Jeff and Flavio's vineyard near Castello Brolio.

While interested and aware of the murder, Bianchi informed them that the murders by the Monster were a top priority to law enforcement at present. He added that the Gotelli murder could very well be the work of the Monster. The fact that the Vineyard murder weapon, a .22 caliber pistol, was a strong reason to suspect the Monster, who had always killed using such a weapon.

Mattaruchi again lived up to his reputation and leadership talents by offering to help form a volunteer investigative committee to assist on the vineyard murder case while Florence police continued their priority of investigating the Monster. He would be chairman of the voluntary group.

Since the beginning of the string of Monster murders 18 years ago, the Florence police force had found itself short-handed in its investigative efforts. With respect and confidence in Mattaruchi, Bianchi accepted his offer—a ground-breaking move for a local police agency to permit an outside person to assist in investigative work.

While Mattaruchi would be the actual chairman, Deputy Commissioner Bianchi would oversee the investigative committee. Bianchi was legally responsible for assuring that the committee's work upheld proper police practices.

Bianchi already had his work cut out for him with the Monster murder cases. A massive, frustrating investigation was already underway in Italy to find perhaps the most shocking murderer in all of Italy. Numerous law enforcement officers were working on the case.

Mattaruchi began organizing the volunteer group while awaiting the final go-ahead. The group was to consist of himself, Jeff, Flavio, and Luigi Acquistapace, Flavio's father. Once Luigi heard about the committee, he eagerly volunteered to help investigate the murder. After all, it was his daughter-in-law Celeste's father. He had extensive experience in the wine industry, having met many vintners throughout Italy over the years.

After a group discussion, they settled on a name for the group. It was agreed to go by the title Comitato Investigativo Volontario, or Comitato, for short.

Although all the members of the Comitato were competent and highly motivated, surely a welcome aid to Polizia, they had to work in conjunction with Italian law enforcement teams. Their official status was only as an advisory group.

Their goal was to assist Polizia by identifying and investigating possible suspects in the Gotelli murder and to create supportive reports on those suspects. They were willing to work without pay, simply volunteering as a public service.

The investigation was intended to operate for only a few weeks at most, hoping to identify potential suspect individuals or groups who might be involved in the newly named Vineyard Murder.

As the Vineyard investigation began, law enforcement continued their work on the bigger issue that had to be dealt with: Central Italy was having a crisis in Florence—full attention had to be given to the Monster investigation in view of the multiple slayings.

Mattaruchi suggested that initially, the Comitato should analyze various aspects of the Monster's work just in case evidence could be found to prove whether Gotelli's murder was committed by him or not.

Bianchi endorsed the suggestion. So initially, they met in Bianchi's office, which was nicknamed 'The War Room.'

Deputy Commissioner Bianchi would be the chairman of the Vineyard murder while overseeing the Monster investigation. He was pleased with the extra help. A massive, frustrating investigation was already underway in Italy to find perhaps the most shocking murderer in all of Italy. Numerous law enforcement officers were working on the case.

The goal of Mattaruchi's committee was simple—to investigate possible suspects of the Gotelli murder and submit reports on potential culprits.

But the opportunity for Bianchi to have a group of dedicated men to voluntarily assist in the recent murder case in Chianti was a no-brainer. All he had to do was monitor the investigation of the volunteers and keep them on the path of legal conformance. He freely gave them the go-ahead to take on the study of the Vineyard Murder case.

Mattaruchi was widely known by most investigative experts as one of the most experienced and motivated police investigators in all of Italy. He offered to devote his time to this investigation for free. What a gift! In this present role, he would investigate the possibility of the involvement of Italian organized crime in the Gotelli murder. The Comitato members chosen by Mattaruchi impressed Bianchi.

All the Comitato members agreed that the priority was thoroughly examining the murders of the key suspect, the Monster. He had murdered ten people in the Florence area, dating back to 1968, leaving absolutely zero clues. This individual, hopefully only one person, had killed randomly with no apparent motive. His methods were frightening, even to the police, who knew certain gruesome aspects not yet made public. Since the Monster was the key suspect, the Comitato would first try to determine for sure if he could or could not have murdered Antonio Gotelli—was there any correlation?

Mattaruchi reminded the committee, "The Monster is already in the sights of intensive police scrutiny. We can initially support law enforcement by giving information and suggestions that we have on him. Then and only then can we move on to the Vineyard case. But we can set up our future agenda for the Vineyard investigation.

Following a couple of meetings, with group participation, the Comitato chose the assignments of each member when it came time to focus on the murder in Chianti.

Jeff Wiler was a former investigative attorney in Alameda County, California, with ten-plus years of experience as a private attorney. He had valuable experience in law and law enforcement. He was assigned the investigation of grape growers and vineyards workers in the vicinity of the murder.

Flavio Acquistapace, another seasoned attorney, and an Italian citizen was asked to look at family members and relatives to see if any relatives may have had grudges or motives contributing to the murder of Gotelli. The assignment would involve possible clues only family members would know, requiring extreme tact and confidentiality to avoid insulting the family. This assignment would prove to be one of the most difficult to take on because Flavio would be prying into the private lives of relatives. It could be insulting to members of his family. But Flavio was an intelligent and tactful man with over a decade of court cases and investigations. Plus, he knew the family best and could tactfully pursue questioning on topics the family might find delicate. He agreed.

Luigi Acquistapace volunteered to investigate various wine producers in Italy to see if any might have possible motives to act against rival vintners. Luigi's years working for Nino Negri Winery in Lombardia and his knowledge of the industry throughout Italy could be valuable in identifying potential motives to act against competing vintners. Not likely, but his knowledge could be helpful, and his enthusiasm was refreshing.

Within a week, the Comitato group was given the go-ahead to officially organize, with Mattaruchi supervising and Bianchi overseeing.

They set a schedule of periodic meetings at the Osteria Vecchio Vicolo (Old Alley Tavern), a historic restaurant, calling the sessions

"Summit Meetings." The tavern was just steps away from the historic Ponte Vecchio (Old Bridge) over the Arno River in Florence—one of the most recognized symbols of Florence. It is not far from the Uffizi Museum in Florence.

The five men began meeting at the Osteria Vecchio for cocktails, discussion, and dinner. Located in a Renaissance-era palace once owned by the Medici family, Osteria Vecchio is fine dining for craft cocktail enthusiasts, with stellar service to match an extraordinary décor. The avant-garde cocktail lounge boasts towering shelves of alcohol and an undercurrent of experimental flair.

At the afternoon sessions at the Osteria, Jeff would sometimes order a Manhattan, his favorite cocktail. Mattaruchi and Bianchi would kid him about his American cocktail. Jeff responded that he had a secret recipe to make the drink at home, but when questioned about the ingredients of his homemade Manhattans, he refused to reveal the ingredients. From then on, the men referred to it as his 'Jeff-hattan.'

Jeff responded to the jest with a proposal to those working with Mattaruchi,

"What do you say we change our boss's name to something simpler. From now on, let's just refer to him as 'Chief Matt', what do you think?"

The others nodded in agreement. Except one. He just slowly put his chin down, then lifted it with a smile.

At the outset of the investigations, 'Chief Matt' emphasized, "The motive is key, as it always is in such crimes. So far, the field of suspects is unknown, with no names."

But he went on to raise the possibility that, although the Monster was the first to be suspected, mainly because the weapon was a .22 caliber pistol, there remained doubt that he was, in fact, the culprit. There were a few markedly different circumstances.

1. All six of the Monster murders were located within 20 miles of Florence. The Vineyard murder near the Castello Brolio was 42 miles from Florence. Why so far from his past crimes?

2. A pistol was found in a dry creek bed near the Vineyard murder scene, with no prints. Experts were able to verify it was the weapon that fired the shots killing Gotelli. Why was the pistol left at the scene?

3. The shooter missed the up-close target multiple times and emptied the weapon. It didn't sound like the gunman was experienced.

4. No mutilation was found.

The committee discussed the points that seemed to point away from the Florence Monster. But, in the larger picture, the likelihood of him being the culprit had to be more fully examined. Public paranoia was growing, and demanded it be explored exhaustively.

Even if the facts later point to other possible conclusions, the major attention must first be directed at the Monster. A leading newspaper had said, "Gotelli was shot with a .22 caliber pistol, just like the weapon used by The Monster."

The outcry of the people required the investigation of him to be given top priority.

CHAPTER 4

A WORLD OF MURDER

Jeff and Flavio became engrossed in the investigations of both Gotelli and the Monster, looking for any possible connection. After all, they were attorneys, and practicing law was their chosen livelihood. They found criminal investigations fascinating. Both of their wives supported them in their chosen careers.

Flavio asked when they could begin their separate investigation. As Jeff awaited the formal go-ahead for Mattaruchi's Comitato to begin their informal investigation, he recalled the recent newspaper report of the Migliorini-Mainardi murder that frightened daughter Suzy. The shocking article in the Florence newspaper, La Nazione, on June 20, had prompted her to call home.

Deputy Commissioner Bianchi informed 'Chief Matt' that the police had determined that the murder weapon was a .22 caliber weapon, most likely a pistol.

Further, the female victim had been mutilated, a piece of evidence withheld from the public.

Mattaruchi told the Comitato that Gotelli had been shot three times, also with a .22 caliber weapon. There were no known witnesses. While the killing was brutal, some people were not shocked. Gotelli had stepped on many toes as he moved up the ladder at CNI Shipbuilding. Then he launched his selfish intrusion into Chianti, provoking a group of grape-growing farmers.

Nevertheless, the news of his murder generated dismay and fear among citizens in Florence and Genoa. Such atrocities had been almost commonplace in places like Sicily, Rome, and New York—but appalling in an agricultural setting such as Chianti. The crime had all the characteristics of an assassination—bold and professional.

By now, Jeff and Flavio had become absorbed in the investigation of Gotelli's murder. Both of their wives and family wholeheartedly supported their efforts to help solve the mystery of the tragedy. They canceled all their proposed travel plans,

Flavio desperately wanted to help with the investigation but found it difficult to devote much time to it while his wife's family grieved. However, he stayed connected with Jeff and Mattaruchi and pitched in when he could. 'Chief Matt' sensed Flavio's frustration and counseled him to stick close to his family for the time being and be patient. Soon enough he would be given other assignments to help in the investigation.

Jeff was eager to participate in the current murder case and he made sure that Mattaruchi had notified the Polizia about his experience as a prosecuting attorney and his affiliation with the high-level Polizia boss earlier,

That being the case, he was anxious to begin the investigation, but he had to be patient and wait for the volunteer committee to join.

As he waited, he pondered the details of the Vineyard killing. Questions began to come to mind.

Who would have known Gotelli was coming to his vineyard that day? How did the killer or killers know he would be there at the vineyard at a specific time?

Gotelli himself must have told someone. If so, it must have been someone he thought he could trust, a family member or a co-worker.

His own family, especially his wife, must have known of his trip, but who else? Maybe one of his children or someone he worked with? Did Gotelli or a family member mention it to others at his work? And if so, who? The shooter must have been tipped off—unless the killing was a spur-of-the-moment unforeseen act, which is remote. It seemed more likely that it was premeditated. The details of the crime at such a remote place seemed as though it was planned.

The wife or one of the children may have told someone of Gotelli's trip to the vineyard.

There's a good chance other vintners had seen him at the vineyard earlier that day.

Maybe on a previous trip to the vineyard before, he met someone who knew he was coming back.

Thinking it over, Jeff assumed that Gotelli's visit that day was spontaneous, not a scheduled meeting with someone. Yet the question remained: How could the shooter plan the murder unless the killer knew he was coming?

The question of the caliber of the murder weapon came to his mind—why had a low-caliber weapon been used? Because it was quieter? Easier to hide?

He took some time to briefly research this topic and concluded that the use of a .22 caliber weapon is not a rare choice. The simple truth is the fact that many citizens, particularly farmers, have .22 caliber guns. Why? Because small predators and rodents are sometimes present in vineyards and farms, and they feed on the crops. Farmers shoot them to keep their populations down.

*   *   *

Porcupines, for example, are rodents that commonly eat buds, various fruits, and vegetables such as carrots, melons, potatoes, and a selection of berries. They also damage grape vines. Their teeth are designed to chew and feed on both soft and hard plant material. They can strip the bark off grapevines. Their occasional bark diet has made them unpopular with grape farmers and owners of ornamental trees.

There are other reasons why a farmer in Italy might want to carry a pistol: snakes and vipers.

A snake is a legless reptile of the sub-order Serpentes with a long, thin body and a fork-shaped tongue.

A viper is a venomous, or poisonous, snake in the family Viperidae. Seven species of vipers exist in Italy. Why wouldn't a farmer want a pistol in his pocket while traipsing through his fields and vineyards?

Vipers are not easy to love.

*   *   *

Jeff became more intrigued as he ran through the few potential suspects.

How about that young man who drove Suzy to the country road and wanted to park? Should he be considered a suspect? He seemed to have disappeared.

Then he speculated—did Gotelli have a silent partner? Maybe he had an unknown partner who turned on him. Certainly, several people objected to his ruthless business tactics.

The larger the puzzle, the more his interest grew. He made one strong decision—the murder was inconsistent with those of the Monster. But he would leave that challenge to the ongoing investigations by Polizia. His instincts told him to concentrate on other potential perpetrators.

As he pondered, he realized he loved a challenge and tried to direct his attention to other possibilities. He recalled his experiences of ten years ago—the burst of adrenaline, the excitement of dangerous work, and, yes, even the fears that were part of such times.

Who could gain by knocking off Gotelli? He thought of the mobs that came to mind: the Frisco mob, a Sicilian mob, or any other ones, for that matter —would any of them want a share of the wine market in Chianti badly enough to murder for it? For that matter it could be anyone wanting to break into the wine business.

His gut feeling was this murder didn't fit the 'modus operandi' of organized crime. There didn't seem to be a strong motive—they had had no interest in farming or the wine business in the past. They concentrated more on other organized crime 'businesses' of the past.

What about the mysterious lady who had accompanied Gotelli to Chianti earlier? Since she was close to him, she might know who a possible suspect could be.

So many possibilities. Where does it end? At this point, Jeff had reasoned himself into a corner.

He knew there was little use in devoting so much time to an investigation that had not even been sanctioned to begin yet. He must wait for permission from Mattaruchi to begin the investigation of the Vineyard Murder. 'Chief Matt' will get us started soon enough once he gets permission from Polizia.

In the interim, Jeff decided to read up on other famous criminal cases in Italy that made worldwide headlines. Perhaps he can learn something from them.

He spent much of the day at the Florence Library going through sensational murders of the recent past, hoping to learn some explanations from previous crimes—those reported in newspapers from the past.

He found a few articles that were in recent years and were eye opening. They illustrated that murder is all around the world.

*   *   *

THE LUDWIG GROUP

Wolfgang Abel, born 25 March 1959, and Marco Furlan, born 16 January 1960, were German-Italian serial killers who were arrested for a series of murders in Italy, the Netherlands, and Germany between 1977 and 1984.

The two met in high school, soon agreeing on the need to clean up the world of everything that, in their opinion, was "deviant" including prostitutes, homosexuals, drug addicts, "sinful" priests, homeless people, and red-light cinemas. Their relationship continued beyond school and into adulthood. The two members were both sons of the upper middle class in Verona, Italy. They were responsible for ten confirmed murders in the late 1970s and the early 1980s. Some victims were burned alive.

They claimed innocence, saying they were scapegoats for a police force that could not find the real criminals.

THE KIDNAPPING OF CIRO CIRILLO IN SOUTHERN ITALY

The Italian Red Brigades, Brigate Rosse, was a militant left-wing organization in Italy that gained notoriety in the 1970s and 1980s for kidnappings, murders, and sabotage. Its self-proclaimed aim was to undermine the Italian state and pave the way for a Marxist upheaval led by a "revolutionary proletariat."

On April 27, 1981, the Red Brigades kidnapped the 60-year-old Christian Democrat politician Ciro Cirillo and killed his two-man escort. They threatened to execute Cirillo unless the government accepted certain demands, including a ransom. It refused in the past.

None of the political demands of the Red Brigades were met, and, in the end, they accepted that a ransom was enough to release Cirillo.

While this event was not directly related to the Gotelli Murder, it demonstrated the widespread presence of violence and crime in general. There were many serious crises in Italy in the 1970s and 1980s. Law enforcement agencies had many cases in many locations. The resources were stretched thin.

THE ATTEMPTED ASSASSINATION OF POPE JOHN PAUL II

On 13 May 1981, in St. Peter's Square in Vatican City, Pope John Paul II was shot with a Browning Hi-Power rifle and wounded by Mehmet Ali Ağca while he was entering the square. The Pope was struck twice and suffered severe blood loss. Two other people were wounded, also. Ağca was apprehended immediately and later sentenced to life in prison by an Italian court. Several years later, the Pope forgave Ağca for the assassination attempt. He was pardoned by Italian President Carlo Azeglio Ciampi at the Pope›s request and was eventually deported to Turkey.

Oddly, another attack against the pontiff took place one year later, on 12 May 1982, in Fatima, Portugal. A Spanish Traditionalist priest who opposed Vatican II reforms, and saw Pope John as a perpetrator of them, was stopped before he attempted to attack the Pope with a bayonet.

This happened five days before Suzy Wiler started her wine seminar in Florence.

* * *

Jeff gained a lot from those cases: there is a lot of chaos out there—some big, some small. But there are many, different motives. He learned that not all have predictable motives. He centered himself with an open mind—to use logic and persevere.

He was getting 'pumped up' on the upcoming investigation by Mattaruchi's group.

He decided to zero in on the Monster first, starting with a prior year's murder by him.

He dropped by Mattaruchi's office to chat about his thoughts. He was hoping the Gotelli investigation would start soon. He expressed his eagerness to get started. 'Chief Matt' understood Jeff's anxiety and assured him that it would not be long. Further, he didn't see anything wrong with a low-key investigation starting early, but only a gathering of information and potential subjects of study.

Mattaruchi was pleased with Jeff's enthusiasm and contacted Deputy Commissioner Bianchi, requesting permission to allow Jeff to review police records on the Monster murders. Permission was granted.

Jeff went to work immediately. What first caught his attention was the fact that there were five Monster murder cases dating back to 1964 and as late as 1982. Then, each case had a newspaper report as well as a file of each police investigation.

While reading the reports it became apparent that some facts were not included in the newspapers. That was logical because unpublished clues kept the assailant ignorant of the investigation's progress.

Each case was extremely interesting and at the same time, upsetting.

Case 1: Barbara Locci and Antonio Lo Bianco – Shot to death on the night of 21 August 1968.

Locci, a native of Sardinia, had a reputation in Florence for her sexual promiscuity, receiving the nickname Ape Regina (Queen Bee). She and her boyfriend, Lo Bianco, had driven to the outskirts of Florence with her six-year-old son Natalino sleeping in the back seat. While they were romancing, Locci and Lo Bianco were shot. And, reportedly, an unknown man carried Natalino to a house about a mile away. The police report stated the murder weapon was a .22 caliber Baretta pistol.

Stefano Mele, Locci's older husband, later confessed to the crime and was charged with murder and sentenced to 14 years in prison—a light sentence because he was deemed mentally infirm. He later retracted the confession. But, after six years in prison, another couple were murdered with the same gun.

Following an anonymous tip, the police reexamined the evidence from this closed case. They found that the gun used in the 1968 case was the same one used in the later1974 Monster murder—the bullets were from the very same pistol. Stefano Mele could not have committed the later murder in 1974—he had been in prison the whole time. He was released.

After reading the report on Mele Jeff could see that no clue pointed toward the Vineyard Murder. It gave zero evidence that could be helpful in Gotelli's murder.

He moved on to review the next case.

Case 2: Stefania Pettini and Pasquale Gentilcore—Shot to death on the night of 14 September 1974.

Teenaged sweethearts Stefania Pettini age 18, an accountant, and Pasquale Gentilcore, age 19, a barman, were shot and stabbed on a country lane near Borgo San Lorenzo, a town in the mountains about 19 miles north of Florence.

They were close to a notorious discothèque called Teen Club, where they were supposed to spend the evening with friends.

Information withheld by Police: Pettini's corpse was undressed, violated with a grapevine stalk, and disfigured with 97 stab wounds. Further, police theorized that the killer was impotent and acted out of rage or sexual dysfunction. And, out of respect, they also withheld from the newspapers the fact that the murdered couple had been having sex in their parked car.

Case 3: Carmella De Nuccio, age 21, shop assistant, and warehouseman Giovanni Foggi, age 30, were fatally shot and stabbed on 6 June 1981, in their parked car near Scandicci, where the engaged couple both lived.

De Nuccio had undergone post-mortem genital mutilation. The killer cut out her pubic area with a notched knife, a fact police had withheld. Both bodies were discovered outside the car the next day.

Before the discovery of the bodies, and before the subsequent newspaper report of the murders, a young voyeur, paramedic Enzo Spalletti, age 30, spoke about the murders before the corpses had been discovered. And the word of this reached Polizia.

Most young people in Italy live with their parents until they marry. Many marry late. Some of them engage in the pastime of having sex in a car. This climate invites spectators who hide and watch the action. In Italy, there are a number of these voyeurs, called 'Indiani' or Indians. Some of them even carry microphones or night cameras.

Spalletti was charged with murder and spent three months in jail before the actual perpetrator struck again, four months later, thus exonerating him.

Additionally, a big break—they discovered the pistol had a defective firing pin that marked each shell. They elected to withhold that fact plus, they refrained from giving the specific details of the mutilation of Carmella's body.

'Good news on the firing pin defect' Jeff thought. 'That could help all the cases.'

'Still, nothing to link to the Vineyard Murder.'

Again, Jeff saw nothing in the way of a connection he was hoping for.

Case 4: Susanna Cambi, and Stefano Baldi—shot on 23 October 1981.

Not only were they shot, but both had also been stabbed in a park near Calenzano. Suzanna's pubic hair had been cut out in the same fashion as the previous murder victim. A few days before the murder, Susanna had told her mother that somebody was tormenting her and even chasing her by car. An anonymous person phoned Cambi's mother the morning after the murder to talk to her about her daughter. No incriminating motive was discovered, and no one was ever arrested.

This case investigation had some unique and welcome findings: two bullet shells were found next to the victims. It was the first and only time the police found spent shells at a Monster murder scene. They analyzed them and discovered that both victims had been shot by the same .22 caliber Beretta pistol, with Winchester bullets, series H.

∗   ∗   ∗

The ability to compare ammunition is a direct result of the invention of rifling (the arrangement of spiral grooves on the inside of a rifle barrel) around the turn of the 16th century. By forcing the bullet to spin as it travels down the barrel of the weapon the precision is increased. At the same time, the rifling leaves marks on the bullet that are indicative of that barrel.

∗   ∗   ∗

There was one other piece of evidence that was withheld: a men's size 44 boot print had been found next to her body—a large size, matching a size 10 1/2 in the United States

'Maybe we are getting somewhere,' Jeff thought. 'Maybe we will be able to either dismiss the Monster from our case. Or maybe find a connection.'

'And now, his latest attack.'

Case 5: Antonella Migliorini and Paolo Mainardi—shot on 19 June 1982

They both were shot in Mainardi's car on a provincial road in Montespertoli by a .22 caliber Beretta, again with a defective firing pin. They were not mutilated, and police believed that the road was busy, and the shooter did not have time to mutilate the female victim. The murder took place between 10:00 and 11:00 p.m.

Police speculated that after shooting the couple, the killer drove Mainardi's car for a few meters to hide it with the bodies in a woodland area nearby, only to lose control of the car and abandon it in the ditch.

Another possibility was Mainardi may have heard or seen the killer approaching and attempted to drive away, only to lose control of his car and drive into a ditch on the other side of the road.

Several passing motorists had seen the car parked at the side of the road with its interior light turned on.

Again, ballistics revealed the weapon was the same as the prior murders.

Just after that fifth murder event on June 19, 1982, an envelope arrived at the police station. Inside was a newspaper clipping from 1968 about the couple who had been shot and a suggestion to reexamine the case. Someone was aware of the connection. Was it a taunt sent by the murderer?

Were the actions of the killer becoming more reckless? He seemed panicky, as shown by driving the victims' car into a ditch and his inability to molest the female victim.

Over the course of the investigation, over 100 people had the honor of serving as suspects. Among them were not only Enzo Spalletti, the voyeur, but there was Francesco Vinci, whose car was discovered in the woods near the site of the latest murder. He was taken in but was released when the next killing occurred while he was still in custody.

Later, an anonymous letter accused Pietro Paccini. He had killed a man who was seducing his girlfriend in 1951 before raping her next to the corpse and he had a reputation for being over-sexed and beating his wife and daughters. He was arrested and pronounced guilty, but it was later appealed.

Despite a robust number of leads — from fingerprint evidence to eyewitness accounts, police sketches and several inconsistent theories— no killer was ever arrested. Eventually his killings stopped. The men's size 44 boot print found at one murder scene was never matched to a suspect. Some of the candidates suspected of being the Monster of Florence may have already died, but the killer's identity was never found. He may still be out there. If so, he would probably be in his late seventies by now.

Police ballistics had shown Gotelli was not shot by the weapon used by the Monster. It was still possible that the Monster committed the crime with a different weapon, but most all the investigators felt it was not the case.

Such is the case with the Monster of Florence, who started his reign of terror in 1968 and continued into 1982. The exceptionally brutal murderer targeted couples in the hills near the city and killed ten people over the years—so far.

Jeff was glad to hear the news that the Vineyard murder may not be the work of the Monster.

The hunt for the Monster has a long one. Although Jeff felt the Vineyard murder was not the work of the Monster, he still had to wait for the formal report by Florence Polizia.

He still had a haunting fear—he could be wrong. Maybe Gotelli was just in the wrong place at the wrong time. Maybe he used a different weapon.

'Gads', he thought. 'I'm just going with the odds. I don't think the Monster did it. We'll see for sure with the Polizia report.'

'What do they have to say?'

CHAPTER 5

THE MONSTER

.

While murder is as old as recorded history, there is a particularly brutal, or heinous crime of murder that has erupted and found its place recently in post-World War II Italy, specifically near the metropolis of Florence.

Because murder is reported almost daily in the newspapers and other media, virtually everybody throughout the world is aware of the presence of individual murderers. But a murder spree is another thing. Like an epidemic, it must be given top priority as soon as possible with every available resource.

Homicide is a term used to describe the killing of one human being by another.

Manslaughter is killing someone in a spontaneous event, such as a sudden loss of temper on the spur of the moment, unplanned.

Murder is the intentional killing of a person by another and is not legally justified or excusable. It is distinguished from manslaughter by the element of premeditation. A murder is considered a homicide, but homicide can also refer to a justifiable or excusable killing.

Those initially chosen to investigate Gotelli's murder all agreed that the priority had to be a thorough examination of the Monster murders. The murders were too shocking to postpone. In a fourteen-year span, ten people were murdered in four separate events—two people each time. The incidents were thoroughly investigated, and although none were solved, the evidence proved the murderer or murderers were the same. And, at this point, several suspects had been arrested, but none were proven guilty. To law enforcement in Florence murder investigations became the top priority. It became an obsession, to the detriment of other cases with less publicity. Polizia looked at the spree as a mockery. They felt helpless.

The shocking factor with the Monster's murders is the length of the spree. As each case grew cold, the spree seemed to be over. And then he would strike again. In each case the news report of the murder was brief, mainly because the police held back aspects of the evidence in hopes the killer would not learn of any clues or mistakes he may have made.

The killing of Antonio Gotelli in 1982 was plainly a murder—and the initial suspect was, in the eyes of most, The Monster of Florence.

Gotelli's flaw was that he was ruthless, and perhaps a threat to someone—but to whom? Had he stumbled upon the killer who was about to take another life? Did he know something about the identity of the Monster of Florence? Was his murder revenge or random?

Then Jeff rationalized: "Let's say Gotelli's murder proves to be just another by the Monster. He had by then murdered ten people in five separate murders around Florence over the past few years and has left few clues. This individual, hopefully only one person, was killing people without specific motives. His methods are frightening even to the police. That investigation had to take priority over most others.

"What can we do," Jeff mused, "to nail this Monster, to prove he killed Antonio Gotelli? Or find that he didn't?"

Jeff reviewed news articles about the murders by The Monster in hopes of finding details that might help in the upcoming investigations by the Comitato.

He also thought there should be a plan to also investigate Gotelli's business associates and contacts, seeking to establish good alibis and eliminating possible motives and clues. He was pretty sure that 'Chief Matt' would be anticipating those investigations.

Just 15 months after the almost-botched murders of Antonella Migliorini and Paolo Mainardi, the Monster struck again. But he again failed to achieve full "success."

There were several theories about the Monster of Florence, one being that he might be cracking as time passed. Regardless, Jeff realized he must keep track of all possible clues concerning the Monster or any other possible suspect. He knew this was the best path to follow as the Comitato waited for full approval to start their formal investigation.

With all the publicity of the horrendous murders by the Monster of Florence, it is likely that, in most people's minds, the Vineyard Murder of Antonio Gotelli was the work of the Monster. After all, a murderer using a .22 caliber pistol is rather unusual—especially where similar murders occurred near Florence. It is considered a pocket weapon.

Jeff realized, like most citizens of Florence, that the Monster of Florence was the most likely suspect. He couldn't deny that the key linking piece of evidence was the .22 caliber gun used in every single murder, including the Gotelli murder.

"It's gotta be him," he thought, but "why would a serial killer use such a small weapon?"

It's hard to comprehend, but all six murders by the Monster were committed with a .22 pistol. On the other hand, small-caliber weapons are relatively common—and they can inflict a wound that will more than ruin one's day.

*   *   *

On March 30, 1981, John Hinckley Jr. shot and wounded U. S. President Ronald Reagan after a speaking engagement at the Washington Hilton. He was nearly killed by a single .22 caliber round within an inch of his heart. The pistol bullet had ricocheted off the side of the presidential limousine and hit him in the left underarm, breaking a rib, puncturing a lung, causing serious internal bleeding. Hinkley had fired a Röhm RG 14 .22 LR blue steel revolver six times in 1.7 seconds, missing the president with all six shots.

The first round hit White House press secretary James Brady in the head above his left eye, passing through underneath his brain and shattering his brain cavity. Upon arrival at George Washington University Hospital, Brady was close to death but was stabilized in the emergency room, then underwent emergency exploratory surgery. He survived but had brain damage and was permanently disabled. His death years later was considered a homicide because it was ultimately caused by his injury.

Reagan, as he was being wheeled into the operating room, sought to project a positive demeanor, saying: "I hope you are all Republicans!"

*   *   *

The idea of a murderer using a small caliber weapon does not defy logic, but it is rare in most assassinations. In the case of Gotelli's murder, it clearly does not fit.

Other factors seemed to point away from the Monster of Florence. Facts known only to the investigative team turned their thinking to someone other than the Monster. For good reasons:

1. Law enforcement had made a valuable discovery: in one of the Florence murders two shells were found at the scene, coming from a single weapon, a .22 caliber Beretta pistol, with a defective firing pin marking each shell.

Most handguns, aside from revolvers, eject the shells after firing. If the shooter doesn't go to the trouble of retrieving them, they can become evidence. In the Monster Murders no weapon was ever found, but the police lab reports revealed that the same pistol had been used in two separate Monster murders, one last year, 1981, and one earlier in 1974.

It was a .22 caliber handgun. The firing pin on that weapon had a small defect that left unmistakable marks on the rims of the cartridges, as unique as a fingerprint. The weapon itself has not been found.

2. The pistol that was found in the Vineyard Murder was a Rigarmi 2.75" barrel .22 LR caliber with a seven-round clip. It was a black pistol with ivory color plastic grips and a left-side lever safety. The weapon holds seven bullets, maximum.

When found, there was one bullet in the chamber, three bullets in the victim—shot point-blank, and six empty shells were on the ground, close together. Two of the casings had partial prints on them. The prints were small, like those of a small person or a child.

There was no defective firing pin on this weapon.

3. Six shells were found at the Vineyard scene, and only two had been found at the one Monster murder scene. There were no prints on the Monster site. The prints did not match any in existing police files.

4.   Gotelli's bullet wounds were made up close. Close-contact gun-shots fired from close range leave tell-tale marks called 'stippling tattooing'—marks that are discolorations of the skin caused by burning gunpowder. Gotelli's body had those marks. None of the Monster murders has ever revealed such marks.

5.   A ballistics test of the Vineyard murder showed a different .22 caliber weapon than the ballistics at the Monster-shooting sites.

6.   The killing had no sexual molestation nor mutilation as had the Monster killings, nor was it located in a location known for "necking."

7.   The car tracks did not match any others at the Monster murder scenes.

8.   The Vineyard Murder was 42 miles from Florence. All 'Monster' killings were within 12 miles (19 kilometers) of Florence.

9.   In most of the Monster murders, the female victim had been mutilated—a fact withheld from the newspapers. That did not happen in the murder of Gotelli. It was a significant difference.

10. The size 44 boot print found at the Cambi – Baldi murder scene was a larger size than any of the current suspects.

With widespread paranoia throughout Tuscany, the Monster investigation would surely continue. But now, a separate investigation of the Vineyard Murder in Chianti could be broadened and continued with a clearer focus.

The Italian president in 1982 was Sandro Pertini. He had been elected President of the Italian Republic in 1978. He displayed considerable energy and vigor, playing a major role in helping to restore the public's faith in the government and institutions of Italy. He openly denounced violence and vigorously opposed organized crime in Italy. He was active against the Brigate Rosse terrorism period of the Anni di Piombo, that time of upheaval years earlier.

Pertini actively met with other national leaders and encouraged trade and travel in his country. In March of 1982, he hosted a meeting with President Reagan.

One can imagine the pressure on Polizia while the highly publicized murders of the Monster of Florence continued—especially the murders of Antonella Migliorini and Paolo Mainardi in Chianti on the nineteenth of June that year.

*   *   *

At that point, crime investigation was a decade away from discovering an awesome tool to assist in identifying specific individuals, through DNA testing. DNA (deoxyribonucleic acid) later became a very essential molecule, found in almost all organisms. It contains hereditary material in our genes—things that make us unique. It is the carrier of genetic information.

It is present in the cells of our sweat, blood, skin, hair, mucus, saliva, urine, and other bodily sources. It became extremely useful in tracing family trees, verifying heritages, victim identification, and other purposes, including crime investigation.

Later, DNA testing was to become valuable in identifying suspects by comparing a sample of their DNA to that found at crime scenes. It can also be used to exclude suspects in crimes such as rape cases and other serious crimes. It is useful in identifying victims of mass disasters. In later years it was to have a profound impact on the criminal justice system. It proved valuable following the 9/11 attacks of 2001.

But it was not around to help in any murder cases in 1982.

*   *   *

At this stage in the investigation of the Gotelli murder, the Monster of Florence was ruled out as the perpetrator. Evidence discovered in the Gotelli case overwhelmingly pointed to a different culprit.

Later years revealed more murders by the Monster of Florence. The concern by investigators of the 8 murders of the past was only to be intensified. He was never to be apprehended after committing several more murders until his last, in 1985. In a period of 17 years, the Monster was to commit 16 known murders in all.

Many theories about his identity remain—the most bizarre being the theory that he was part of a Satanic cult that provided sacrifices for black magic, or a devil worshipper who used body parts in worship and orgies.

How did the same gun with the same set of bullets appear in similar yet very different crimes that occurred over five years apart? Why did the Monster wait so long between his killings.

He faded away, much in the fashion of Jack the Ripper. The criminal who came to be known as The Monster remained the most wanted and most heinous murderer in modern history in Italy. The time had come to move on to the Vineyard murder separately.

The debates over the separation of the Gotelli murder from the investigation of the Monster murders could have gone on for a long time. But the dilemma for the police was whether to devote valuable time to the Vineyard Murder, a remotely possible Monster case, or move on to the much higher priority. They were convinced the two cases were separate— they chose to continue with pursuit of the Monster separately. Fortunately, the presence of Mattaruchi's investigative team was a key factor.

Of course, there were exceptions to this general formula. Wilhelm Friedrich Horst Meyer and Jens Uwe Rüsch, victims of the fifth crime, were both men, though it is believed that Rüsch's long hair fooled the Monster into thinking he was a woman. In the 1974 homicide, Stefania Pettini's vagina had been stuffed with a grapevine.

While morbid, it would be interesting to know the murderer's thinking when he discovered his targeted victim turned out to be a male.

At this point Florence police concluded that the Gotelli murder was not the work of the Monster. The decision was not made public but was shared with Mattaruchi's investigative group, including the withheld facts.

The Monster was ruled out of this case, but he had more murders ahead of him. Polizia backed off the Vineyard Murder at this time, knowing the Comitato would pursue the case for the time being. The horrific path of the Monster of Florence would continue.

In Florence, Italy, from 1968 to eventually 1985, there were at least 16 known homicides by a single killer—the Monster of Florence. Ten at present, six more to follow. He was bold and seemingly impossible to track down. He was one of the most prolific murderers in modern history.

The go-ahead was given to the Comitato.

They were eager.

CHAPTER 6

THE GREEN LIGHT

The prospect of eliminating the Monster from the Vineyard Murder investigation was a relief to those awaiting the go-ahead to pursue the Gotelli case.

But first, Jeff felt there was one more person who needed to be checked out. In Jeff's mind, there was someone who may have slipped between the cracks in the Monster investigation. A person who was near the Monster murder of June 19. Someone only Jeff was aware of.

The man he was thinking of was the young guy who made a pass at Jeff's daughter Suzy that night: Giovanni Mazzina. A quick contact with Suzy and with the Accademia revealed no information about his whereabouts at present. The Accademia refused to give Jeff the man's residential address.

At the next meeting of the Comitato, Jeff brought up Suzy's evening date with Mazzina. He had taken Suzy to a location close to the scene of the June 19 Mainardi-Migliorini murders near Florence. And he should be contacted and questioned. It's possible he may be the notorious Monster.

Jeff explained, "I know we received permission to move on to the Vineyard Murder, but before we do, I think we should investigate Giovanni Mazzina first. That night he was in the vicinity of the Monster's murder with my daughter, and we should check him out on both murders—Monster and Vineyard. For all we know, the Monster may be right under our noses. Mazzina had taken the wine course earlier with Suzy, and he could be a possible suspect in the murder of the Chianti vineyardist Gotelli. It would be a logical move to interview him."

Mattaruchi and Reneo Bianchi agreed that there should be an investigation of him, and he should be located and questioned. Because Mazzina had been a student at the wine seminar, the Comitato gave the assignment to Luigi Acquistapace. Luigi was the committee's wine expert, and he knew people in the wine world, many in Tuscany.

Luigi began by contacting the Florence Wine Accademia to find information on Mazzina. He brought a legal order prepared by Polizia, authorizing the release of personal information.

Any mention of a murder in the Florence area at this time was taken very seriously by everyone, especially an entity as prestigious as the Accademia. In this case, the institution complied and was ready to help in any way they could. The director sat down with Luigi to review Mazzina's class record.

Mazzina had left Florence on the weekend when the wine seminar finished. His file indicated that he resided in the southern city of Positano.

Luigi was able to contact him by telephone and explain the investigation. Mazzina understood the need for a meeting to discuss it further—especially since he might be a suspect.

At Mazzina's request they met in Rome since he had already planned a trip there earlier.

They met at a caffetteria in Rome, a couple of blocks from the Trevi Fountain. Over a cup of coffee, they discussed Mazzina's actions and travels since that tragic June 19 day.

Why had he studied winemaking in Tuscany? Because it was the most renowned wine region in Italy, if not the world. He explained the desire to produce wines in the vicinity of his home in the south. He lived in Positano, not far from Sorrento.

He had high hopes of a successful career in winemaking in the vineyard region south of Naples. He was more of a vineyardist than a commercial winemaker.

He admitted he had made a pass to Suzy, his classmate, on that night of the murder, but was rejected, and took her back to her school resident room as she asked.

He had been embarrassed but insisted he had not done anything illegal.

At Luigi's request he produced evidence of his recent travels, including travel receipts and copies of purchases with his signature. The records did not prove anything about the Monster murders, but at least Mazzina was being cooperative.

Luigi reviewed the details of the Monster murder and found some key points:

Based on police reports the murder was committed between 9:00 p.m. and 10:00 p.m., based on testimony of witnesses interviewed by Polizia. They had found the car which contained the bodies, stuck along the side of the road.

Mazzina had taken Suzy back to her lodging at 11:30 p.m. the night of the Monster Murder. Her room at the Accademia was 25 miles from the murder scene. There is no way he could have committed the Monster murder of June 19

Following Luigi's report, Deputy Commissioner Bianchi cleared Mazzina as a Monster suspect, and they eliminated him from the list of Gotelli murder suspects, as well. Now, with that last phase wrapped up, the Comitato Committee could devote their full attention to the Vineyard murder case.

But where should they start?

Could someone connected with the shipbuilding company CNI be involved? Gotelli had fought hard to succeed in the firm and possibly had made some enemies. He was the company president's nephew. Maybe his placement had quashed someone else's hopes of advancing to that high-level position.

Were the potential suspects in the wine industry? Possibly growers or vintners?

A plan of action was needed—to look at one suspect at a time.

Starting with growers, one name stood out immediately: Bruno Pellegrini.

He had been a big help for Jeff and Flavio because he oversaw their vineyard while they were in California. He knew the two of them had invested in purchasing the vineyard with plans to spend time there during retirement. He seemed to like them and their goals.

Plus, they had paid him promptly when something needed repair or other costs he incurred to maintain the vineyard. They were friends.

But he did surprise them with his verbal attack on Gotelli and realtor Furielli. He did have a temper, and maybe it was the trigger for an explosion of aggression. If nothing else, he should be investigated to hopefully exonerate him.

So, the vineyard maintenance man Bruno Pellegrini was the initial suspect. And he had confronted Gotelli two months before the murder.

When he learned about Gotelli's plan to undermine the other growers in the Gaiole area he confronted him. He and Gotelli had an angry exchange shortly before Gotelli was murdered. He had openly said to others that he hated him and had even driven to Radda to chastise the realtor who had helped Gotelli buy the vincyard in their domain.

But Pellegrini was in Rome when the shooting occurred, a fact backed up by the hotel records where he stayed at the time. Further, the one firearm that he owned, a .22 caliber pistol, passed a ballistics test, proving his weapon was not the murder weapon. Further, the shell casings that were discovered at the murder site with partial fingerprints were not Pellegrini's. He was taken off the suspect list.

During a following Committee meeting, the conversation moved to the possibility of a person or organization in the wine industry being responsible for the murder. The idea of a grower being responsible did not seem likely, but a wine producer or syndicate could be possibilities. Wine is big business. A grudge or major threat to an existing enterprise could evoke some form of retaliation—and it wouldn't be out of the question that an existing entrepreneur could have taken such a drastic move.

On that topic, Luigi Acquistapace tossed out a name that he had recently heard of, a wine "big shot" from Sicily who had relocated to Chianti. The man's name was given to Luigi by an old friend, Ricardo, who owned a local gift shop in Florence. Earlier, Ricardo had worked at the same winery as Luigi—Nino Negri Winery, located in Lombardi. Ricardo had moved to Florence a few years ago and opened the gift shop.

Since Luigi had come to Florence to serve on the committee, he decided to drop in and visit Ricardo at his shop. In their conversation, he told Ricardo about his assignment on the Comitato.

Ricardo was quite interested in Luigi's assignment and told him of a character he had recently met and learned "enough to not care for the man."

The man was Rico Rizzo —a rather boastful businessman who had built up a wine business in Tuscany with the idea to eventually take advantage of the more lucrative business of making Super Tuscan wines, which had become the rage of Italy.

Rizzo was Sicilian and seemed to think he knew more about the wine business than everyone else. He bragged that he planned to make his mark in the wine business in Chianti.

He ran a small wine shop in Florence to showcase his wines while he looked for a small vineyard of Sangiovese grapes to fulfill his needs.

He had established a small winery several years ago just south of Siena with the idea of challenging the Super Tuscan wines that had burst onto the wine scene. His goal was to use another grape to replace the Cabernet Sauvignon that had been incorporated into Italian wines in recent years to match the wines of France. He learned the Sicilian grape, Nerello Cappuccio, was very near having the characteristics of Cabernet Sauvignon but was much less expensive. It is a grape native to the Etna region of Sicily, and produces a spicy, medium-bodied wine with qualities very similar to Cabernet.

Sicily is the largest wine-producing region in Italy – one that is poised to expand as wine enthusiasts look for new territories and unexpected flavors. A true microcosm of Italy, Sicily can be described as a "viticultural continent". With its 98,000 hectares of vineyards, it leads both Tuscany and Piemonte in wine production.

Rizzo believed that bringing in the inexpensive Nerello grapes from Sicily would eliminate the need for Cabernet, but he still needed a source of Sangiovese grapes to produce the desired "Super Tuscan" blend. Owning a Sangiovese vineyard would provide the heart of the business and blending it with the Nerello would be the ultimate.

Nerello would be the cake, and Sangiovese the frosting.

He had heard of the availability of the vineyard near Gaiole from a contact in Radda. The contact had learned about it through a property listing at Enrico Furielli's real estate office in Radda. Rizzo had sought to buy the vineyard that Gotelli acquired.

Earlier he visited the owner, widow Castagno, on his own and made an offer, hoping she would accept a low offer since she was elderly and had lost her husband a year earlier. She had decided to move out of the area. Rizzo thought he might be able to clinch the vineyard sale—but Gotelli soon arrived and offered a much higher price. Neither Gotelli nor the other vineyardists in the area knew of Rizzo's offer.

Gotelli inadvertently foiled Rizzo's chances of picking up the property at a ridiculously low price. Widow Castagno had jumped at the much higher offer from Gotelli.

When Rizzo learned of the missed opportunity, he was angry with Gotelli's intrusion into his game plan. But now he felt that when the Vineyard Murder investigation wound down, he may still have an opportunity to buy the vineyard.

Luigi sought to meet Rizzo and interview him but first dropped in on realtor Furielli to learn how much he knew about him. The realtor gave his candid opinion: "Secondo me, e' un pallone gonfiato!" ("In my opinion, he is a blowhard!").

Both men laughed, then Furielli continued, "Oh, he's okay, but you know those Sicilians—lots of bravado and bragging. Rizzo thinks of himself as a wine baron, like he's royalty.

"He was a little mad at me for helping Gotelli find the vineyard for sale, removing the opportunity for him to buy it—at a bargain price. He's over it now, especially since hearing of the murder and all the investigations. But he thinks eventually he may have the opportunity to buy that vineyard after all."

"Come on, I'll take you over to his wine shop, and you can ask him questions you may have. I'll introduce you and then leave you with him. Oh, and good luck!"

Luigi spent over an hour talking to Rizzo. Much of the conversation was Rizzo's boastful talk about his achievements and plans. Regarding the events of June 26, Rizzo told Luigi that he had spent that fateful evening in the village of Greve in Chianti at a wine and produce festival 18 miles north of the murder scene near Gaiole. At first, Luigi thought, "Well, maybe . . . but could he prove his attendance there?" Rizzo said he could produce wine sales receipts and invoices of purchases at the festival that night. He showed Luigi the receipts for some of the wines that he purchased that night.

Satisfied with Rizzo's responses, Luigi concluded that he could not have been at the murder scene that night. Following the interview, Rizzo offered him a bottle of Chianti from Greve. He graciously declined.

Later that day, Luigi filed his report with the committee, eliminating Rizzo.

*　*　*

As the number of specific suspects seemed to be disappearing, the Comitato looked toward organizations rather than individuals, possibly wine businesses, or organized crime groups.

The possibility that the murder was related to the wine business was certainly a valid consideration.

Italy was one of the big players in the wine world. At that time, it was a country with one of the highest per capita consumption of wine, second only to Portugal. In both countries wine is most often consumed as an accompaniment to a meal. A wide range of wines are produced to suit all taste preferences.

Wine is a big business throughout Europe, and Italy is one of the larger producers. The Italian wine industry in the 1980s brought in millions of dollars in profits each year.

Is it feasible to consider that professional wine people be suspected of murder?

It is common knowledge that anyone embarking on any business or venture, new career, business, or venture faces possible opposition from existing competitors. Perhaps Gotelli's aggressive entrance into the wine business had been seen as a threat to those already in the field.

Even legitimate producers were known to have taken extreme measures to gain or maintain prominent positions in the wine world. It is very possible that a highly competitive wine businessman saw Gotelli as a threat to existing Chianti producers who currently dominate a large share of a lucrative wine market.

Maybe one or more individuals tried to put the squeeze on Gotelli, and, in his aggressive manner, he brushed them off with threats to challenge them. A confrontation could have evolved into violence.

The members of the Comitato agreed that it was possible that a northern crime organization being involved was also worth consideration.

Recently a Florence police informant had reported that mob members had moved into the Tuscan wine region with hopes of cashing in on the premier wine industry. It was the last thing the famous wine industry needed in their sacred domain.

At this point in the Comitato's investigation, the obvious questions arose: Was Gotelli murdered by a criminal organization that saw him as a threat to their own operations? Did they have ties to existing wine operations? Was there any chance organized crime was involved?

The Comitato decided to look briefly at the possibility of wine people or organized crime groups possibly being the perpetrators. They were not acting on any information that pointed to that possibility, but with Gotelli's venture into the wine business it should be considered.

It is no secret that in recent years the Italian wine producers had attempted to compete with the more popular French wines. They had set out to boost the sales of their wines and challenge the success of French wines, particularly the red wines.

In France the most prestigious reds were Pinot Noir, Cabernet Sauvignon, Cabernet Franc, Malbec, and Merlot. The French dominated in wines made from these grapes.

Wine drinkers throughout the world would rate French wines as the best. Not far behind, though, were wines from other countries such as Spain, Portugal, the United States, and Italy.

But the French advantage prompted Italian wine makers to challenge the popular French wines with "super" wines of their own. The result was the arrival of the "Super Tuscan Wines."

Their wines were not bound by the traditional wine-making laws in Tuscany, which prescribed specific grape blends, aging regulations, and geographical boundaries. Instead, they introduced a spirit of innovation, often blending the popular native grape, Sangiovese, with international varieties such as Cabernet, Merlot, and Syrah.

The Super Tuscans were new, and soon found a popular niche.

This renaissance in the Italian wine industry opened new doors. Some of those who entered through those doors were ready to exploit the opportunity. Whole new horizons arrived, with more flexible regulations and oversight.

Organized crime members could see the value of owning wine properties and producing wine. There were opportunities in many aspects: vineyard ownership, grape sales, and fewer restrictions on making the wines. It didn't take long for them to step in for a piece of the action.

Many would agree that the Italy wine business had become quite competitive and had attracted a few unscrupulous individuals. These new producers were using cheaper grapes from other parts of the country, and so far, had been successful.

Regardless, wine is a staple of Italy and Italian culture. And overall, it is big business.

The entire Italian wine industry could see the potential for record profits in the future.

That is what attracted Antonio Gotelli. He was boldly seeking a level of dominance of the local wine business at any cost. He looked to grab a large share of the Italian market, especially the varietals Sangiovese and Vermentino, a red and a white. He saw unlimited potential in those two wines.

And, with his aggressive business style, he surely would have posed a threat. Established wine producers would have seen him as a serious competitor.

There is no telling what degree of retaliation he may have set off, but it undoubtedly would have drawn a reaction from existing wine companies. His aggressiveness could be considered a possible motive for his murder.

In the past, wine had not been a major business of organized crime, but the potential was there—and for law enforcement, it should be investigated.

It was apparent that a "hit" on Gotelli would eliminate him as a wine competitor. That motive has been the case in many businesses in many fields, and not only in Italy, but in all parts of the world.

So, in this case, wine lords could very well be suspects, eliminating someone who threatened their 'empire.' If the "hit" was by one or more of those competitors, the list of potential perpetrators could be long, from Sicily to Lombardia, and beyond.

Members of the Comitato continued to search for information that might show motives by wine people, possibly pointing to potential suspects. They discussed different scenarios, but nothing concrete surfaced. No information or tips were found to implicate people in the wine business.

Inquiries to other police agencies, underground contacts, and a review of past history gave no credence to the crime they were investigating. Nothing seemed to point towards those in the wine industry.

They agreed to put the possibility of wine people on 'back burner' while they briefly weighed the idea of organized crime being involved in the murder. They work in many fields, depending upon the opportunity and the money at stake.

Although there was no evidence to point to mob people. Italy has its share of mobs. They operate in almost all fields.

To Mattaruchi, a man familiar with several crime families, only one came to his mind—the Comasina Crew, named after a neighborhood in Milan. It was a criminal group that was most active in the 1970s but was still an organization to be reckoned with.

They controlled several neighborhoods in Milan. At one time, they set up roadblocks manned by the gang's members to rob citizens. A few times, they robbed policemen and often mocked them.

Jeff and Flavio glanced at each other when the committee brought up the subject of the Comasina. The two men communicated without words. Memories came back from ten years ago when they were threatened by those organized criminals. The name Comasina Crew was permanently etched in their memories.

Later in California in 1973 they formed their law practice, Jeff and Flavio vowed to avoid any case that even came close to dealing with organized crime.

Now, with the possibility of dealing with them again, their faces reflected similar thoughts:

"Uh-oh, here we are again!"

*   *   *

Ten years ago, Jeff and Flavio had participated in an investigation of fraudulent immigrations by organized Sicilian gang members to and from the United States. It was the investigation where they met and worked with Italian investigator Amadeo Mattaruchi. During that operation they had learned about the criminal gang, the Comasina Crew.

They both had thought that they had heard the last of the Comasina bunch.

After that earlier investigation, the boss, Renato Vallanzasca, was arrested and is still in prison in Milan.

The present-day gang is but a shadow of its former presence. But it has been under casual surveillance up to the present day.

*   *   *

The follow-up investigation of the Comasina was brief.

The Comitato discussed the possibility of the Crew being involved in the murder. But the recent surveillance and lack of major criminal activity over the past four or five years led 'Chief Matt' to advise the Crew to be dropped from the Vintage Murder investigation. There appeared no obvious motive and the crime was far away from their customary turf.

It just was not a feasible avenue to pursue.

CHAPTER 7

SUSPECTS

Now where should the investigation go? There are many questions in deciding that. 'Chief Matt' called the Comitato members together to plan their next move—and where to focus.

He had called them to give updates on their investigations and to plan their next strategy.

"Well," Mattaruchi said, "There is no obvious path to take, so let's go back and learn more about the family. There might be something we overlooked. We can review Gotelli's family records, and his will, and then interview the family again, starting with his widow Caterina.

Since she is ill of late, we must be tactful and not alarm her.

So here is the plan. I will personally interview the mother, Caterina, myself. With her illness and obvious depression, I don't think it is a good idea to have Jeff or Flavio interview her. Also, I want to find out more about her son, Gianni. I know there is something amiss with his relationship with his stepdad.

It should be okay for Flavio to interview the three children, Celeste, Domenico, and Gianni.

We should delve more into her children's lives—interview them again to see if they can suggest any possible enemies of their dad."

It turned out that the report by Flavio was perhaps the most fascinating to the members. He had been assigned to question Gotelli's immediate family, looking for any possible connection to his assassination.

Flavio had volunteered to question the family's children to possibly uncover significant information that might signal a motive or clue related to Gotelli's murder or eliminate them altogether. He volunteered for that role knowing it would require a certain amount of tact and the family's trust.

His request was approved because he was the son-in-law of the deceased Gotelli, and he was someone with whom the family would feel more comfortable in discussing sensitive family issues—being more likely to fully "open up" to him. He wasn't all that knowledgeable about the backgrounds of his in-laws, but one of his top strengths was tact.

He made sure his family interviews were private and low-key. The three children understood the need to investigate all aspects of their father, Antonio Gotelli. Flavio handled the assignment gracefully. It was his goal to be calm and supportive. The entire family understood the need for proof of their information, dates, receipts, and supportive documentation.

But when interviewing son Gianni, he found him to be somewhat bitter. He indicated his stepfather had treated him poorly and not as an equal to his siblings. It was somewhat awkward for Flavio to interrogate his brother-in-law, so he kept the interview simple and brief. He reported the outcome to 'Chief Matt'.

Mattaruchi was about to visit the mom, Caterina, and decided to include a conversation with Gianni to assess if there was a conflict between the father, Gotelli, and the stepson.

Two days later, Mattaruchi contacted Caterina Gotelli at her home in Genoa and tactfully explained that they were continuing the investigation to hopefully find a clue that might ultimately help reveal her husband Antonio's killer. She was very depressed with the state of her health but cooperated with him as best as she could.

'Chief Matt', a master of tact, assured the lady that he needed her help in solving the murder of her husband. His questions to her were pointed at putting her at ease. She was relaxed and pleased with his sincerity. There was nothing accusatory in his line of questioning.

He brought up the subject of her son Gianni and his unhappiness with his father. Caterina acknowledged that fact and explained the conflict between the boy and his stepdad. She then said, "If he is suspected in any way, then I think you should meet with him and clear the air."

Mattaruchi said, "That's very positive of you. It might not be a bad idea. If anyone suspects him in any way, we can clear him immediately. What do you think?"

"I have no doubts that you will clear him, Mr. Mattaruchi."

The following day, at his mother's request, Gianni met with the Police Chief at his mom's house.

The young man reached out to shake hands upon his arrival, and said, "Glad to meet you. I hope this will clear me if I am a suspect."

Mattaruchi liked that, and thought, 'The man looks pretty squared away, to me.'

The mother left the room so the two could talk.

The interrogation was relaxed and went well.

In discussing his family background, Gianni related a series of events that included his past. Mattaruchi learned that Gianni had earlier met with a cousin, Tommaso, a while back.

They had met in Milan previously after Gianni had searched for his mom's relatives. He hardly knew them, as his real dad died when he was a year old. He had found Tommaso, a cousin whom he met for the first time.

Then Gianni recalled,

"I'm not proud of this, but I told Tommaso that I hated my stepdad.

After we met, we went to a bar a couple of times, and, well, I groused about my continuing bad luck, and that I may lose my inheritance if my mom who has cancer died before Antonio. Tommaso appeared to be sympathetic and asked what the eventual estate would be worth if my stepdad died. I didn't know for sure but guessed upwards of three-quarters of a million dollars."

"Then, a week or so later, Tommaso called me and wanted to meet me at the bar again in Milan. He got right to the point, and asked if they were to arrange for me to receive a third of my mom's estate, would it be worth 50 grand to me?"

I asked how they could do that. He said they have ways!

"I looked at his expression as he nodded, as though saying "You know."

"Well, I don't like the sound of all this. Let's just drop it."

Tommaso interrupted, "We just want to take care of you. We can talk more later."

I said, 'No way, I don't want to hear any more about it! On this topic, we are finished, period!"

And we were finished. I didn't want any part of him or anyone in the Vallanzasca family.

Upon hearing the findings, Mattaruchi said, "Wait a minute! That Tommaso guy's surname is Vallanzasca?

"Well, well. If that just doesn't take the cake!"

He was glad he met and interrogated Gianni. It helped the case.

Later, at a meeting of the Comitato, 'Chief Matt' shared the name with the members.

Jeff asked, "You knew the name?'

"Oh yeah, I knew the name, all right—Renato Vallanzasca. You should remember that name yourself. He was the former boss of a Milan gang, the Comasina Crew, remember?

But something's wrong. As you know, we investigated them in 1972. Then, after you returned to the States, we eventually took them down six or seven years ago. Vallanzasca is still in San Vittore Prison in central Milan, along with about 600 other losers."

Jeff then recalled the name of the mobster, the gang's boss in the Comasina neighborhood of Milan.

It was learned that Flavio's mother-in-law Caterina was, in fact, a Vallanzasca, but she had taken on Gotelli's surname years ago when she married Antonio Gotelli. The reason: not only to please Gotelli but also to avoid the unacceptable notoriety of her Milan gangster brother, Renato Vallanzasca, whom she despised.

Jeff called Flavio and updated him on the findings about the family. Flavio was surprised to learn there was a link to the Milan mob they investigated in 1972.

"Oh, my God," Flavio said, "that's my mother-in-law's former surname?"

No one had ever told Gotelli that his wife was the sister of the head of the Comasina Crew.

So, an immediate investigation of the gang was launched to see if it was still an active gang.

The investigation of the Comasina Crew found they still existed in Milan. The former leader was Renato Vallanzasca, who had been arrested eight years ago and was still in prison. But he had a younger brother, Tommaso, who was age 40. He was the one who had made the proposal to save Gianni's inheritance.

While son Gianni was not overly close to his dad and could be a possible suspect, he was deemed innocent by the Comitato. Further, he could present proof that he was in England at the time of Gotelli's murder. He produced records of his flight ticket and pointed out the long-distance telephone call that his brother Domenico made to inform him of the murder. Italian police investigators proved that he had been on the appropriate plane—a fact that Flavio ascertained without an embarrassing interview.

As the investigation proceeded, sisters-in-law, Celeste, and Sofia had daily telephone conversations, and in one discussion, Celeste referred to Gianni Gotelli as her stepbrother.

Sofia asked, "Why do you call him your stepbrother? Isn't he your brother? He is a Gotelli, isn't he?

Celeste said, "To us, he is our brother, but technically he is our stepbrother. Our mother, Caterina, earlier was married to a man named Alfonso Musso. He died in 1944. I thought you knew that."

Sofia asked, "But his surname is Gotelli, so why isn't he Gianni Musso?"

"Well, Dad didn't want the surname Musso kept because it's too close to Mussolini. He wanted Gotelli instead. And mom agreed, and from then on, she used Gotelli as her married name too."

Sofia asked, "Then why didn't she just go by her maiden name, as most Italian women do when they marry?"

Celeste responded, "Well, I guess she just wanted harmony in their marriage in 1946 and went by the surname Gotelli to please Antonio. Some women do that in Italy, as you may know."

Sofia then asked, "Does Flavio know Gianni is your stepbrother?"

"No, I don't think so. All our relatives just accepted Gianni as Antonio's son. And we three all love our mom, Caterina, dearly."

"So, it's not a secret?"

"No," Celeste said, "there just wasn't any reason to advertise the difference. Gianni is our brother, and we love him."

That evening Sofia passed the information on to Jeff.

The investigating team immediately went to vital records of Milan. They came up with the name of Gianni's father, Alfonso Musso, and Gianni's birth record of 1943. And one more surprising fact: the mother's birth name is Caterina Vallanzasca. She went by the surname Gotelli after marrying Antonio Gotelli in 1945.

They soon learned that there had been a connection between Gianni and Tommaso Vallanzasca. Gianni had gone to Milan to meet Tommaso because they were blood relatives, cousins. Gianni's mother, Caterina, was the sister of Renato Vallanzasca.

They questioned Gianni, who admitted to the friendship but claimed he had no clue about Vallanzasca's actions. They had met when Gianni first moved to Milan and, out of curiosity, set out to find his mom's relatives. His mom, Caterina, told him long ago that she wanted nothing to do with her gangster brother. Gianni had gone to meet cousin Tomasso without telling his mother. The two young men occasionally met in a coffee shop and discussed family history.

Two police detectives were sent to investigate Tommaso Vallanzasca in Milan. He had a minor criminal record for car theft and shoplifting, but those offenses were ten-plus years ago, and he was not considered dangerous. Those who knew of him considered him more of a big mouth than a criminal. He had, in fact, tipped the police off on a couple of break-ins in recent years. He had a good alibi for the date of Gotelli's murder. He was in jail that day for drunk driving.

It did not appear that the "local" mob was involved in the murder. The Comasina gang had ceased to be a dominant factor. They were small-time crooks now.

What's the story? All suspects have iron-clad excuses for their where-abouts when Gotelli was murdered. Who is left? Was it a murder coordinated by several people?

As difficult as it seemed, it was time to closely examine the immediate family.

Flavio presented his findings regarding the family.

The additional findings were rather tedious—nothing shocking. Like most families, the Gotelli family had a few facts that others need not know. The other data found was rather mundane, except for the background of Gianni. Flavio offered his findings:

The family tree for Antonio Gotelli showed that he was born in 1920, and his wife, Caterina, was born in 1918. It was his first marriage and her second.

In 1940, Gotelli's wife, Caterina, married Alfonso Musso in Milan, Italy. They had only one child, Gianni Musso, born in 1943. Caterina was widowed when Alfonso died unexpectedly in 1944. She then married Antonio in 1945 and became Caterina Gotelli. They soon had a daughter Celeste, born in 1946, and a son Domenico, born in 1948.

Antonio Gotelli was proud of his daughter and son. Ten years ago, in 1972 Celeste married Flavio Acquistapace, a successful U. S. attorney. Son, Domenico, was still single, and had a promising career with the CNI shipbuilding firm. To Antonio, the two were very successful and very respectable—he bragged about them.

But Flavio had learned Gotelli's love for his stepson Gianni was not the same for his son Domenico and daughter Celeste. Few people knew Gianni was Gotelli's stepson, or that he had been slighted over the years. The two never got along well.

When Gotelli later made his will, he insisted his estate would go to his son, Domenico, and daughter, Celeste. Nothing to Gianni.

At the following Comitato meeting, Flavio shared the report with all members of the investigative committee.

Jeff asked Flavio, "Why would Gotelli favor the younger son, Domenico? Isn't it traditional to favor the oldest son?"

Flavio answered, "Yes, but I learned a lot when interviewing Domenico. He had emphasized that he truly cares for his older step-brother Gianni.

He told me the story of changing Gianni's surname to Gotelli, that it was previously Musso, and that he was worried because it was close to Mussolini, it might damage his business image.

Because the older Gianni was his stepson, not his blood son, Gotelli favored Domenico and Celeste over him.

In Italy, inheritances usually go to natural children, often the oldest son—but normally not to a stepchild. And in this case, Gotelli never really accepted Gianni as a true family member. He often belittled him. Most people had assumed that all three children were Gotellis since they all had the surname."

After the members showed questioning looks, Jeff said, "Well, with the insensitivity of his stepdad, it's pretty evident why Gianni moved to Milan. He found work as a bank teller and chose to live there instead of in Genoa. His sister, Celeste, had told me he hated his stepfather. I can understand that."

Then Mattaruchi added, "He did not tell his mother, Caterina, that he had looked up her nephew in Milan, a cousin named Tommaso. After all, the two were blood relatives through his ailing mom, Caterina."

They went on, discussing the facts that they had learned.

Gianni had met with the cousin a few times to learn more about that side of the family. After all, he had found work in Milan and felt connected with family for the first time. He never told his stepfather Gotell of his connection to his mom's family, only that he became employed there.

When Gianni told his mother about the meetings with Tommaso, Caterina, became quite upset. She told him of the criminal activities of her brother, Renato Vallanzasca, who had been the boss of the criminal organization in Milan, the Banda della Comasina, known simply as the Comasina Crew. Renato had been put in prison ten years ago. She directed Gianni to discontinue the affiliation with that side of her family and to keep that information to himself. She had not even told her husband, Antonio, of her relationship with the Vallanzasca family.

Gianni followed his mom's advice. He now was certain he wanted no part of her brother's family.

Jeff asked, "Well, that was good, wasn't it?'

"Yes," Mattaruchi said, "indirectly." Then he paused, waiting for the others to catch up.

"Poor Caterina was just trying to put her three children on an equal basis as far as their eventual inheritance was concerned."

"According to Gotelli's wife, Caterina, her husband developed Restrictive Cardiomyopathy, a heart condition, a few years back."

"What's that?"

Mattaruchi said, "It's a term for a relatively common heart condition,"

* * *

Restrictive Cardiomyopathy occurs when the tissues of the ventricles become rigid and cannot fill with blood properly. Eventually, it may lead to heart failure. It is more common in older adults and can result from infiltrative conditions involving the accumulation of abnormal substances in bodily tissues, such as amyloidosis —not serious. Still, it is something to be aware of.

* * *

"With that development," Mattaruchi continued, "Caterina decided to revise her will. She took all three children aside and secretly told them that in the event of her husband's death, she would become the owner of the entire family estate. She had met with her attorney and prepared her own personal will, which read that in the event of her death, the estate would go to all three children in equal shares. Her goal was to correct the inequity her husband had created.

She wanted them to know that the estate would be divided three ways equally upon her demise. But that was only if her husband predeceased her."

Then recently, she informed the children, one by one, that she had come down with cancer, insisting on their silence for the time being.

Mattaruchi related that she had not considered the possibility that she might die first, but a twist of events showed up a couple of years later, just before her husband's death: Caterina had been diagnosed with hepatocellular carcinoma: liver cancer.

* * *

The disease is often called hepatoma and is the most common type of liver cancer, accounting for 75% of all cases of liver cancer, officially hepatocellular carcinoma, and is known as primary liver cancer. It is the seventh most common cancer in women globally and the third most significant cause of cancer-related death.

In 1901 German physics professor, Wilhelm Conrad Roentgen received the first Nobel Prize awarded in physics. Later, in France, a breakthrough occurred when it was discovered that daily doses of radiation over several weeks improved the patients' chances of a cure. The methods and the machines that deliver radiation therapy have steadily improved since then.

But it was not enough to save Caterina.

* * *

Caterina was given several months to live. She told no one at first. She was not only shocked by her diagnosis and prognosis but was worried about what the impact of her passing first would have on the entire family. She doubted her husband's ability to hold the family together. She had been the counselor and advisor for their children over the years. In their minds, she was the family's peacekeeper.

Mattaruchi explained that, weeks earlier, she had released the news of her condition, to only the three children. All had been upset with the news of her impending demise.

"A couple of days after the announcement, Gianni realized the predictable impact of her death—no more protection by her and probably no eventual inheritance for him."

"But," 'Chief Matt' continued, "what Gianni had said to me next during our interrogation was a good indication that he had not been involved in the murder of his stepdad. He told me he rejected his cousin Tommaso Vallanzasca's proposal of a 'hit' on Antonio Gotelli."

"No way," Gianni had said to Tommaso, "I don't want to hear any more about it! On this topic, we are finished, period!" The Comitato concluded that Gianni should be removed as a suspect.

The research and interviews ascertained that all the family members could prove their whereabouts at the time of the murder. In several ways, it was a learning experience for Flavio and Jeff. The Gotelli family had not traveled often to the United States, so most contact with them was during annual vacation trips by the two families—brief contacts.

Gotelli's wife Caterina was in Genoa on the day and evening of Saturday, June 19. She was at a theater in Genoa, following a shopping day with a lady friend. Daughter Celeste had still been in California before traveling to Italy.

They produced receipts backing up their whereabouts.

Further, Caterina had nothing to gain with the loss of her husband. She was already wealthy and quite content with her status in society.

Flavio's wife, Celeste, was moderately wealthy and had everything she could want. With such a successful husband, she was quite content. Still, he requested physical proof of her day and evening events. She understood the need.

Caterina's son Domenico had worked at CNI in Genoa, confirmed by upper management. His reputation might have been damaged by the fact that he was investigated, but he was already an heir to the estate and had a promising career. There appeared to be no motive for him to murder his father since things were already going so well for him.

The next day Jeff met with Mattaruchi and Reneo Bianchi. They all agreed on the need to retrace their paths of investigation. They must have overlooked something.

Since no legal actions involving wills or inheritances were found, Investigators were satisfied that no family members were involved in Gotelli's death.

But things had not fallen in place so far, and one evening Jeff filled Sofia in on the progress of the investigation and mentioned that the case had reached an impasse.

"It doesn't make any sense," Jeff explained. "There had to be a motive for the killing, but all the possible leads have been explored with no plausible reason for the murder."

Shaking her head, Sofia said, "Logical clues must have been overlooked. A murder like this does not just happen. It was in a remote area. How did the killer know Gotelli was there? Shell casings were found at the scene and did not match any found in the Monster murders. I would be surprised if the Monster would have made that mistake here. It had to be premeditated. Someone must have known Gotelli would be at the vineyard, at that location, and at that time."

She paused and gave Jeff a long look. "The investigation needs to move back to people close to Gotelli, not the mafia. And no other growers—it would have been too foolish for them to commit the crime in their own backyard." It had to be someone who knew Gotelli well—not strangers, someone who knew of his travels. At least, that's how it seems to me."

Jeff looked at his wife and was taken aback by her logic.

"You are right," he said, "We have to go back to square one."

At the next meeting of the Comitato, the members were rather sedate, lacking new ideas.

They had earlier thought that the investigations of the family and the Comasina Crew might lead to solving the case, or produce new possible suspects, but that was not the case.

Then Jeff recalled that earlier Flavio had an interview with Gianni who gave some surprising information, saying that Gotelli had a "lady friend" on the side. Gianni had seen them in a booth together at a tavern in Genoa a couple of years earlier. They were being "very familiar," he said. The lady was one he had seen before at CNI, where she and his stepdad worked. In fact, Gianni knew her son, Ernesto Delucchi, who had also worked at CNI. Flavio recalled that he had mentioned it to his wife, Celeste. She admitted she was aware of the relationship. Her brother Gianni had told her that he had seen their father flirting a few times with a much younger woman. Celeste had decided to keep it to herself, as she felt it would be painful to her mother. She figured the affair was simply a temporary thing.

Jeff then thought back to the Radda realtor who them about the woman seen with Gotelli.

Mattaruchi immediately jumped on the news. "We should check her out. It would be helpful to know Gotelli's whereabouts and actions just before the murder."

CHAPTER 8

STUNNER

The investigation was not producing any meaningful progress at this point. The Comasina Crew was not the active organization it once was and was removed from the investigation. There were fewer members than in earlier years, and most of the members were aging. Nothing in the investigation pointed to them.

Nobody came forward with information about Gotelli or his actions that resulted in his murder. No one was able to reconstruct his actions those last few days before he was shot.

Flavio, having learned more about his father-in-law than he wanted to know, suggested to Jeff that the two of them try to track down the mystery lady. If anyone might know the secret activities of an unfaithful man, it would be his lover.

So, the two decided to do a little sleuth work privately—not wanting to upset the grieving family.

Jeff contacted Enrico Furielli, the realtor whom he had met earlier in Radda, and described his investigation. He asked where Gotelli might have stayed on his trips to Chianti. Furielli said that while he and Gotelli were looking for a suitable vineyard for sale, the two of them remained in close touch. Gotelli stayed in a hotel close to the vineyard that he wanted and ultimately purchased.

The realtor looked at his sales file and located the name, phone number, and location of the hotel, Villa Capannelle. With that information, Jeff asked Flavio to go to the hotel, explain the investigation, and inquire about Gotelli.

Flavio's trip to the hotel proved quite revealing. On arrival at the Villa Capannelle, he showed his credentials from Polizia and explained the reason of his visit.

Although he knew much about the history of the Gotelli family, he found surprising information about his father-in-law, Antonio: He had indeed taken a lover!

Flavio was lucky in finding out that the lady who had earlier accompanied Gotelli to the hotel a couple of times, had recently returned alone for an overnight stay.

The hotel clerk had the credit card information giving the woman's name, contact number, and address. He described her as attractive and said she paid the entire bill and arranged transportation for herself, hiring a local to drive her the 42 miles from Gaiole to Florence. She was to fly from Florence to Genoa.

She had checked in on June 26 and checked out on June 27.

Flavio gasped: Gotelli was murdered on the evening of June 26!

This must have been Antonio's girlfriend, whom Celeste told him about.

Her name was Mirabella Nicolini.

With further investigation Flavio learned more about her.

She was employed at CNI eight years ago, in 1974. She soon became a valued employee, and after three years became Gotelli's private secretary. She remained his secretary until 1980 when he retired.

From some of the CNI employees he discovered that Gotelli had taken her as a lover five years ago, just three years before his retirement from CNI.

When Flavio learned that her son Ernesto also worked at CNI, he contacted him for an interview.

Ernesto admitted that his mom sometimes went on 'business trips' with Gotelli. He admitted he was worried lately because he was unable to contact her. Further, she had become an alcoholic and he was concerned about her whereabouts.

Two days later Flavio received a telephone call from Ernesto, who was quite nervous and asked to meet 'as soon as possible.'

Ernesto had tracked his mother down. She called him and through questioning he learned where she was. She had holed up in Gotelli's apartment at the airport in Genoa. He immediately drove to the airport and found her.

She was in a drunken state and the apartment was a mess of dirty clothing, scattered newspapers, glasses and silverware and several empty Amaretto and Grappa bottles. Her eyes were swollen, and she cried intermittently. It was difficult to understand her with the slurs between the tears.

He took her to his apartment in Genoa and cleaned her up as best as he could. Then, with assistance from his church priest, he was able to check her into a care facility where she could receive treatments for recovery.

Staying close to her, he soon learned of her tragic actions.

Shaken himself, he ultimately made the difficult decision to turn his mother over to the authorities.

He learned of the Mattaruchi committee and arranged for his mother's surrender. He was heartbroken at turning his mother in. He was permitted to be present at the formal interview by the Comitato.

The interrogation was conducted in a calm and compassionate manner—no anger or demands. There was no threat from her. She was timid and frightened.

Mirabella, at age 49, was 13 years younger than Gotelli. She was an attractive widow with a grown son from an earlier marriage.

Shortly after she was hired into a clerical position at CNI, she set out to get ahead in the organization by any means necessary. She was able to manipulate people, even her supervisor, with her good looks and ambition.

Earlier she had worked as a secretary at the Fiat Automotive factory in Torino (Turin), Italy, during the "Hot Autumn" period in Italy that began in the summer of 1968 and involved a series of strikes as workers demanded a flat rate pay rise. Italy erupted as thousands of workers went on strike.

* * *

The strikes occurred during a major weakness within the Italian government. The Christian Democracy had been in office for 20 years. An economic slump led to the "hot autumn" of 1969, a season of strikes, factory occupations, and mass demonstrations throughout northern Italy, with its epicenter at Fiat in Turin. Stoppages were led by workers and militant leftist groups. The protests were not only about pay and work-related matters but also about conditions outside the factory, such as housing, transport, and pensions, and they formed part of a more general wave of political and student protests, including opposition to the Vietnam War.

Workers demanded wage increases and the same conditions as white-collar workers within the company. The protests were also a scene of major violence as some protests drew the hostility of the police. A strike against high rents outside the factory gates at Corso Traiano in Torino was attacked by the police and led to a running battle with the police.

The overall chaos produced several economic actions by major industries, including layoffs.

*   *   *

Mirabella subsequently lost her job. She returned to the Genoa area in 1974 and resolved to turn things around.

She soon landed a secretarial job at CNI. She set out to slip into company social circles and assume the politics of moving upward. With her good looks, she was able to attract the attention of her male co-workers and management. It wasn't long before Gotelli fell under her spell. And, within months, she was selected to be his personal secretary.

It was not long before co-workers backed off from confronting her. It was apparent that crossing her would be looked at as crossing Gotelli.

At present, she had been his mistress for 5 years, unknown to most people. He had also been giving her money occasionally and keeping her in a separate apartment in Cornigliano Ligure, seven kilometers west of the center of Genoa. He also had a private apartment near the Genoa airport where she sometimes stayed with him when he went on business trips.

The only other person Gotelli told of his apartment was his son, Domenico, with strict instructions to keep it confidential, for privacy reasons when traveling. He never told him of his romantic interludes there.

In the past year he had taken her to Florence a couple of times, and recently to see his new vineyard in Chianti.

It was about this time that there came a point when her appeal began to wane. He was growing tired of her assertive behavior. She apparently failed to respect his authority.

Over the past year she acted a bit reckless and was drinking too much. In his mind, she was becoming an alcoholic, posing a potential scandal for him.

Earlier he had promised to marry her but lately he appeared to be backing out. Mirabella was extremely distraught when Gotelli broke his promise that he would divorce his wife.

On his next upcoming trip to Chianti, he told her he was fed up with her foolishness and told her she could not join him. During their argument he slapped her and announced he would no longer give her money, and that they were through.

An angry argument ensued, and ended when he told her he would fire her and her adult son Ernesto from their jobs at CNI—a critical loss of income and benefits. Ernesto was her son from a previous marriage to Sergio Delucchi, who she divorced earlier.

Ernesto worried about his mother being single and alone. A few years before he had given her a .22 pistol, because she often traveled to work and elsewhere alone. It was after a gypsy threatened her in Genoa when she refused to give him a handout. Ernesto told her to always carry the weapon in her purse. She had read about the Monster of Florence, who murdered with a .22 pistol. It worked for him, and it gave her a sense of security.

Her son was her pride and joy.

He had proudly chosen to make CNI his career, and losing his job would be a true tragedy for him. Her first reaction was anger.

What should she do?

She had grown to believe that she had strong control over Gotelli, and that he treasured the love of a younger woman. Her dismay was over-whelming, then it turned to rage. After all her devotion to him. And now, 'Arrivederci'? No way! He's not going to just toss me aside!

She'd show him!

He was going to destroy her and her son after all she had done to build a new life. He was going to toss them aside—and she wasn't going to let him get away with that.

He avoided her calls and attempts to see him at work. She was going to get even. But how can she take him on, face to face?

Gotelli had earlier taken her to his vineyard before and after buying it. Now he was about to go again. And she knew how to get there. Perfect! That's where she'll confront him and do whatever it takes to get even!

After their interview with Mirabella, Jeff and Flavio put together enough facts to learn the final explanation. Ernesto was allowed to be with his mother during the interviews with Jeff and Flavio. They compiled the following story given by Mirabella:

Gotelli had a rental apartment near the Genoa Cristoforo Colombo Airport. He maintained it as a convenience when traveling. He would sometimes take Mirabella there for periodic 'rendezvous."

She had a key to the apartment, as he did.

In the apartment, Gotelli had installed a safe, much like a safety deposit box. He had two keys and gave her one—only for emergencies and purchases he authorized. Sometimes when he was away, he would instruct her to purchase something for the apartment, such as food, alcohol, or toiletries.

He often stored extra cash in the box when he made purchases outside of company business—such as gifts for Mirabella and other purchases he wanted to keep secret. Most of the cash was in the forms of lira, pounds, and U. S. dollars. The total kept in the safe sometimes exceeded four thousand dollars to pay for items and services he did not want to show on his corporate account.

Recently Mirabella had given that cache of money a lot of thought.

'That could be a way to get even', she had earlier thought.

She knew the next date he was going to visit the vineyard. She secretly decided to confront him at the Chianti vineyard and tell him she would expose their affair.

✶ ✶ ✶

She arrived late in the afternoon, as the sun was setting. She picked a spot to park under a large tree out of sight from his vineyard. She wanted to be inconspicuous by parking her car in a grove of bushy trees, facing away from the vineyard. It was a good location because she could approach and leave without being seen by others.

Gotelli had not seen her.

It was cloudy at the time, but as the sun inched slowly behind the nearby hills, she could see the outline of his white rental car near the road. She set out to confront him.

She quietly walked the 200 yards to the site of his work. It was silent, except for an occasional low rumble of thunder. She carried her purse with her pistol inside. She slowly approached him.

He was alone, with his back to her, operating a hand-held electric drill. He was working on a wooden door, replacing the hinges. He did not see her until she was 20 feet behind him as he laid down the drill.

She said, "I had wanted to talk to him and give him one last chance to patch up our relationship. I told him that he had become cruel and unreasonable. I asked him what he wanted me to do to get back together again. I said I wouldn't take 'no' for an answer. Something had changed his feelings for me, and I wanted to know why.

He said that I had turned into a bossy drunk, that made him look bad, and he wanted no part of me. Then he cursed and ordered me to leave.

I told him he was cruel and that we had to talk this out now, once and for all."

He shouted, "There is nothing to talk about. Get the hell out of here!" Then he walked to me, slapped the purse out of my hands, and threw me down, and kicked me. Then he stepped back.

"I picked up my purse and stood up, and said, 'You animal! I'm warning you. Stop hitting and kicking me!'

Again, he walked towards me. He was furious.

I backed away and pulled my pistol out of my purse and told him to stop.

He was outraged but kept coming. I feared for my life.

I shot him point-blank, pulling the trigger several times, missing some shots but hitting him at least two or three times. He finally fell to the ground, but I had emptied the gun.

Panicked, I decided to pick up the bullet shells and run back to my car, but . . . "

At this moment in the explanation, Mirabella stopped talking and was shaking for a couple of minutes. Then she dabbed her eyes and continued.

"I was aware that the Monster of Florence, whoever that is, had the reputation of murdering with a .22 caliber pistol. Then I thought that maybe this shooting would be blamed on him!

So, I left the shells on the ground and went to my car. I wiped the pistol and threw it into the nearby creek. I didn't want to be caught with it on my way home.

I returned to my hotel, Villa Capannelle, and spent most of the night crying with fear. I checked out early the next morning, drove the rental car back to Florence and boarded a plane home.

When I got home, I immediately went to our airport apartment. I wanted to remove all items that were mine and anything that might point to me. I took the money in the safe, over two thousand dollars, relocked it, and went to my apartment in Cornigliano Ligure, near Genoa."

"At that point, I lost it. So many things had happened. I curled up in my bed for two days, only getting up for a snack or two. I had absolutely no idea what would happen to me. I thought I would get the death penalty. I was losing my mind!"

During the interview, her son confirmed, in front of her, that she had indeed been "losing it." He looked at her lovingly as she placed her hands over her face. He, too, was frightened.

Her concluding downfall would be her failure to pass a fingerprint test.

What was to be her destiny? Was it the death penalty?

*   *   *

Before the unification of Italy in 1860, capital punishment was performed in almost all states of Italy. After the unification of Italy in 1861, the new Italian parliament promised to reform the repressive and arbitrary prison system inherited from the former absolutist states of the peninsula.

Capital punishment in Italy had been banned since 1889, except during the period of rule by Mussolini, 1926–1945 and shortly thereafter, ending with the restoration of democracy and the adoption of the present constitution on January 1, 1948.

Under Italy's penal code, criminals serving life terms can be eligible for parole after 21 years, if they have a good behavior record.

*   *   *

The partial fingerprints that had been found on the empty shells at the vineyard did match those of Mirabella Nicolini. That pretty much confirmed the evidence against her, although her confession would have been enough to confirm her culpability. She was convicted of murder on

Friday, November 12, 1982, and was sentenced to life imprisonment. She was sent to San Vittore Prison in Milan, Italy.

San Vittore is a prison in the city center of Milan, Italy. Its construction started in 1872 and opened on 7 July 1879. The prison was built for up to 600 male inmates, but eventually expanded to hold as many as 1036 men and women prisoners.

Mirabell, now joined the population.

Her son, Ernesto Delucci, age 30, vowed to visit her at San Vittore once a week.

The prison is the one that still held Renato Vallanzasca, former boss of the Banda della Comasina. He had been imprisoned ten years ago following a criminal investigation in Milan by Amedeo Mattaruchi.

At age 49, with good behavior, Mirabella could be released in 2003, at age 74.

CHAPTER 9
EPILOGUE

Jeff and Flavio took deep breaths after spending the summer in a most unexpected way. What was meant to be a true vacation ended up being a true mystery. They were expecting a relaxing, stress-free few weeks, but circumstances took them elsewhere.

It was a saga that brought the families closer in some ways and reminded them that life can be fragile. Peace and quiet are our destinations but sometimes we learn more by facing stress and danger head on— and often when we do, we grow stronger and learn to value peace and love more.

The mystery of the Vineyard Murder was solved, and the threat was soon conquered. But other mysteries in our world are not solved—ever. The

Monster murders of Florence occurred in the last half of the nineteenth century and continued for over 20 years. The culprit was never caught.

* * *

Fingerprint identification had become an important investigative tool within police agencies in the late 1800s, replacing anthropometric measurements as a more reliable method for identifying people suspected of various offenses. Anthropometric measurements consisted of taking human body measurements such as height, weight, and physical sizes and shapes of human features, limbs, and appendages—data that at times could be helpful, but often found insufficient in identifying specific criminals.

With the introduction of fingerprint identification, forensic investigators universally welcomed it as a reliable identification tool, a huge improvement over the prior methods. It also identified suspects having prior records and those using false names.

Thirty-plus years after the Vineyard Murder, a research group from University at Albany in New York discovered a new technique that identified the sex of fingerprints, i.e., it identifies the sex of an individual based on their fingerprints. The team was led by Jan Halamek, an assistant chemistry professor who based his then-new identification method on amino acids.

It had been discovered that amino acid levels in the sweat of females are twice as high as those of males due to the hormonal differences between the sexes. These characteristics are evident in fingerprints left behind on objects we touch.

It demonstrated that the amino acid content in fingerprints can be used to differentiate between male and female fingerprints.

It would have been a tremendous help in the Vineyard Murder as it would have shown from the start that the murderer was a female.

* * *

Jeff and Flavio and their wives flew back to California on September 8, shortly after Labor Day 1982. They both had much to look forward to—the blessings of their spouses and love of their children, and prosperous careers—better futures, with ongoing love.

Both men have the fortune of good health, prosperity, and happiness with their chosen partners. They had dealt with challenges that might have threatened the love they have of family, but they came out stronger.

At this stage of their lives, they were looking for quieter times—planning for retirement and managing their vineyard in Chianti.

The Wiler girls went on to have successful careers and happy marriages.

Suzy, the wine student, went on to become a marketing manager for a large wine firm in Napa County, California. She was one of the first women to fill that position—and she loves it.

Her sister Laurie went to San Diego State College and studied Marketing. She eventually joined a large clothing firm and proved successful in advertising.

Gina, the natural daughter, only nine years old in 1982, grew to love her grandmother's cooking and eventually became a renowned chef in Napa, California. Eventually she went on to author an Italian cookbook, "Nonna's Best."

Jeff and Sofia were proud of all three girls and made sure they all stayed in close touch. The times of stress were over, and they now bathed in their good fortune.

Both families vowed to stay in touch with their hero, 'Chief Matt' Mattaruchi, who remained in their hearts as another father. He remains their inspiration, and hero.

They all loved their lives in Napa, but also the joys and beauty of Italy. They stayed close to the loving Acquistapace family and visited them often.

THE END

ACKNOWLEDGEMENTS

I give thanks to my friends and family for their encouragement in my work. Along the way, their interest and advice carried me through temporary setbacks and revisions.

Special appreciation goes to two dear friends:

Merrie Ann Marshall helped proofread the pages as I went along, asking pertinent questions and teaching me the value of patience. A dear, she gave me total support.

David Paul, the author of Dare to Care, took time to critique the storyline and technical proprieties of my drafts. He tactfully coached me through several grammatical challenges.

They both helped me to stay on the path of perseverance. Thank you.